KEY WEST SLAM

A Jack Marsh Action Thriller

Mike Pettit

Key West Slam

A Jack Marsh Action Thriller

Edited by CLC Editing Services.

Published by Pettit Publishing on Kindle Format and Amazon's CreateSpace.

Cover designed by Voodoo Graphics

Dedicated to

Robert L. Pettit

The Wind Beneath my Wings

Special Thanks to Cheryl Castela and CLC Editing
for making me look smart.

KEY WEST SLAM

A Jack Marsh Key West Thriller

Chapter 1

The rain began around noon. One minute the sky was marble blue, the next a deep bruised gray. Grape sized raindrops pounded the sidewalks and streets with a million tiny explosions on impact. Locals and tourists alike stood frozen in place letting the huge drops splash them, giving instant relief from the horror of August in Key West. Faces turned upward in deliverance, smiles turned into laughter, then into joy. The streets filled with wet and laughing people, dancing and hugging in wild abandon. Drinkers and partiers from inside the bars joined the impromptu rain dancers on the street. Pedi cabs and taxis leaned on their horns in irritation, for some there was never a break, come rain, sun, heat or cold, the meter never stopped ticking.

Jack took a sip from his tumbler of crushed ice and ginger ale, checked his watch and signaled for Coco to join him.

Coco Duvalier was the Sand Bar's manager and co-owner. She was one of the most strikingly beautiful women Jack had ever seen. Coco was a creation of the Caribbean Islands, a mix of African, Spanish, French, and British. Also, she was the illegitimate granddaughter of Papa Doc Duvalier, the dictator that ruled Haiti with an iron fist for decades. Exiled from the family, she and her mother lived on the streets of Miami where Coco grew up fast and became a survivor.

"Hear anything yet?" Jack asked, as he sipped his drink.

"I'm worried, Jack. Sheila is never late. I sent Lamont over to her apartment, but she doesn't answer her door. Her cell goes straight to voicemail."

"Maybe she hooked up with one of the Rotary people last night. They're in town blowing money like it is water."

The semiannual gathering of the Rotary International meeting for a week in Key West was almost a tradition. A feather in the cap of the state's tourist board and the governors team of mucky mucks.

"She wouldn't do that, not with Mikey at home, Jack. You know that, she would never take anyone home."

"Where's little Mikey? He has to be with her, right? Maybe they drove up to Miami."

"She would have called. I'm calling Bill to see if he can do anything."

"Look, I'm sure Bill's busy with the governor's detail . . ."

"Uh, excuse me. Mister Marsh, can we talk?"

Jack and Coco turned to see a county sheriff's deputy standing to the side, hat in hand.

Jack glanced at Coco quickly, "Sure, what's up, Dave?"

"Uh, we have a situation, Mister Marsh. We have a 10-54 and Sheriff Polk asked me to take you to the sight."

"I'll be glad to go, but where am I going and what the hell is a 10-54?" Jack was puzzled.

"Uh, a 10-54, that would be a *'possible dead person'*, sir."

"A possible dead person! A person is either dead or he isn't, Deputy."

"Yes, sir, and it's a she, not a he, and she is definitely dead."

"I'm going with you," Coco said, as she tossed her bar rag in the sink.

"No way, Coco, you stay here. We both have an idea who it is, there's no need for you to be there. If it's Sheila, I'll call you. Meanwhile, get Lamont back over to her apartment. Break in if he has to. We need to find Mikey."

The ride over to Stock Island was slow going. The rain had created a snarl on Truman Street. Even with the twirling emergency lights flashing, it took forever to reach Roosevelt. Once across the bridge onto Stock Island, Deputy Barnes, swung a hard left onto College and hit the gas. Golfers, ignoring the pouring rain, stopped and watched as the patrol car whizzed by, quickly slowed, and turned onto a crushed coral road that led into a heavy patch of mangroves splashing to a stop in a pothole.

Units from the Monroe County Sheriff's office, the Key West PD and the Navy CID were pulled off to the side of the narrow road. Jack didn't like the blank looks on the crowd of lawmen watching him as he approached. The slickers on the local cops were slippery with rain

"Glad you could make it, Marsh," Sheriff Polk said, sarcastically.

"I was summoned. I am here, Sheriff," Jack answered just as sarcastically, snapping up his raincoat.

There was no love lost between the two men since the shootout on Big Coppitt Key that got a deputy killed and Jack severely wounded. A Cuban Cartel head was holding Coco hostage and Jack moved to rescue her just as the state and county law enforcement launched a full-frontal attack on the compound. The deputy shot Jack in the confusion and then, a moment later, the deputy was killed. Sheriff Polk accused Jack of killing his deputy, but witnesses testified that Jack was unconscious on the ground. Case closed, but not really.

"Come over here and identify the deceased, then I'll want a full statement of your whereabouts for the last thirty-six hours."

"Fuck you, Polk. I'm out of here. If you think I've done something, then you better read me my rights and let me call Jinx before I say another word."

"Jinx," Polk scoffed, "That old drunk. You have a better chance of staying out of jail and lawyering yourself. Now, get over here and tell me who you see."

Jack pushed his way through the thick foliage to where a deputy was standing swatting at mosquitos. Rivulets of rain made their way down the back of his neck raising goosebumps as they rolled. He cursed to himself when his foot sank into the feted mire of the swampy mangrove. The smell slapped him hard, as he bent under a thick hanging vine.

"Jesus, what the hell . . ."

A woman's body was half submerged in a stagnant pool of filth, most of the exposed areas were covered with hermit crabs scurrying over each other fighting over bits of flesh. The left arm had been eaten down to the bone from the elbow to the hand. A submerged swath of sarong swayed back and forth. Jack gagged and turned away staggering back to the road.

"Get that body out of there, Polk. Jesus, man! What's wrong with you?"

"Don't tell me my business, Jack, just give me the name."

"I can't tell from what I just saw. I think it might be Sheila Pollack, one of my girls at the bar. She's missing."

"Missing? Missing from where, Marsh?" Polk quizzed.

"From work, she didn't show up this morning and we are worried about her.

"A bar girl is late for work and you're worried. Yeah right. Cuff him, boys."

"Fuck you, Polk. What the hell's wrong with you? I didn't do this." Jack struggled to free his arms.

"Taze the son of a bitch if he fights you."

Chapter 2

Shark Key sticks out like a ruptured appendage from the Overseas Highway just north of Big Coppitt Key. If you're speeding, like most everyone is on US 1, then you'll miss it. Despite that, Shark Key is where the rich and famous live when they are not being rich and famous in New York, Denver, or out on the coast. Secluded multimillion dollar homes are sprinkled along a road that runs the length of the Key and loops back to the gated entrance. A full-time rent-a-cop patrols the gated community twenty-four seven. If you don't know the magic numbers, you don't get in, if you get in and don't belong, the cop will escort you out.

Max Simms was tired, he had a headache from lack of sleep and he was about to dump the three customers out of his cab if they didn't stop with the mumbo-gumbo. He leaned on the horn again with a burst of ratta-tat-tats trying to get the rent-a-cop's attention.

"Come on, ya mutt, I gotta get back to town," he yelled at the windshield.

He wiped at the fogged windows with a dirty bandana, but the wipers were losing the battle against the rainstorm, so he couldn't see anything anyway. The air inside the taxi was heavy with cheap cologne and booze breath. The guy in the third-row seat passed gas without comment, the other two passengers didn't blink an eye.

"That's it! You fucking guys bail. Get out, this is as far as I'm going. Climb the fucking walls for all I care," Max said, as he popped the lock on the doors. "You guys wanted Shark Key, you got Shark Key, now, vamoose."

"But it's raining," the gas passer said, as if Max wasn't aware of it.

"You from Jersey? Don't you think I know it's raining? Don't you think I got to make a living? I can't be sitting here wasting time while you guys stink up my cab. Humans have to sit back there. I'll have to run it through the wash to get rid of the stink . . ."

Max felt a vice grip close around his neck cutting off his breath.

"Shut up little man and wait. The guard will be here soon."

Max felt his bladder starting to give and he pinched tight, not wanting to wet himself in front of these thugs. He struggled to free himself from the strong hand choking him. He felt himself blacking out and went limp. The hand loosened and he gasped for air, eyeballs wide with fear.

"The fuck you do that for?" He gagged.

"Quiet, my little chicken or I will wring your neck and have Billy's dogs eat you for lunch."

Max rubbed his bruised throat not taking his eyes off the tall thin man with the shaved head and blue eyes. He had a scar that ran down the center of his forehead then slashed back up to his right ear. Max was impressed, to him a scar was evidence that the bearer was not to be messed with.

Max was a coward, he knew he was a coward and wasn't ashamed of it. His cowardice had gotten him out of a lot of jams in Manhattan and here in the Keys. He wasn't afraid to grovel; it was one of his best dodges.

"That must have hurt," he said, nodding at the scar. "Bled a lot, I'll bet."

Scarface ignored him and said something to the other two men. All three laughed at the comment. Max grinned and joined in.

Dark fat clouds scurried low across the sky. The palm fronds were lashing themselves unmercifully in the driving storm, sheets of rain cut visibility to nil. The air in the cab was cloying, heavy with man-odor, Max couldn't stand it any longer and opened the door.

"I'm waiting outside . . ."

He squinted his eyes and braced for the rain as he slid off the seat.

"The fuck," he screamed, as he came face to face with a huge black man in a yellow rain slicker wearing a Smokey Bear hat pulled low.

"What y'all want? Ain't nothing in my logbook about no pink taxi arriving," Smokey said, peering into the van. "Is that you, Mister Marcus?"

"Lupine, Marcus Lupine, Officer."

"Yeah, that's the name I got. Mister Billy been in a sweat for you to get here. Y'all was supposed to be here two days ago."

"We ran into a problem, but it is okay, for now."

"I'm drowning here." Max was soaked, he looked pathetic with his thin hair hanging down over his eyes, his white short sleeved shirt clung to his skinny torso exposing a bull dog shaped tattoo faded with age.

The rent-a-cop looked him up and down, spotted the *'Death Before Dishonor'* tattoo on his right forearm, and asked.

"You in the Corps?"

"Who's asking," Max shot back, rolling his shoulders.

"Desert Storm, '91, *OORAH!*"

"Riker's, '82, *FUCKYA!* Now, let's get this fucking goat cluster going, I'm running late." Max jumped back behind the wheel and put the van in gear.

Five minutes later, Max cut the motor inside a beautifully landscaped compound of tropical flowers, fountains, cut stone circular driveway with an arched portico, and three of the biggest Dobermans he had ever seen. The three dogs sat at attention to the left of the entrance to the Spanish style estate watching, as the passengers climbed out of the van.

"Bring our luggage," Scarface said, as he pushed passed Max.

"Hey, I drive, I don't carry . . . and what about my fare?"

"Bones, pay the man whatever he says we owe him." Marcus snapped his fingers towards one of the other passengers.

Bones followed Max to the rear of the van and popped the hatch. Max's radar was pinging out warning signals, as he stepped to the side. This guy had more jailhouse tattoos than Charley Manson. He even had a swastika cut into his forehead like Charley. Two teardrops were inked in at the corner of his left eye. This guy wasn't to be fucked with.

"How much do we owe you?" Bones pulled an old-style suitcase out from among the other cases and worked the combination.

"Let's see, Key West Bight to Shark Key, tax, mileage and wear, wait time, hazardous weather, miscellaneous . . ."

16

"Just give me a number, old man," Bones barked.

"Let's call it thirty-five even."

Bones popped open the suitcase and Max's jaw dropped. The case was packed with banded stacks of one hundred-dollar bills.

"Uh . . . deadhead back to town doubles the rate." Max said, cautiously. He couldn't take his eyes off the money, but he had been around long enough to know you don't leave money on the table. He was ready to back off if the mutt questioned the excess charge.

"You got change for a hundred?"

"No, too dangerous to carry change. Key West is the murder capital of the Keys, didn't you know. It ain't safe."

Bones smirked as he pulled one bill out of a stack and handed it to Max.

"Keep the change . . ."

"What's the holdup out here?"

Max turned to see who was asking and his mouth dropped for the second time in five minutes.

"Billy Rocket! No shit, is that you?" Max stammered.

Billy Rocket! The Rocket Man was Max's number one heavy metal idol from the eighties. The only group better was Twisted Sister. Rocket had so many number one hits they couldn't be counted. Max owned every one of them on eight tracks, cassettes, and cd's. His glovebox was loaded with them. Marsh and the other guys always gave him a hard time for being such a heavy metal head. They said he should be listening to that sixties and seventies crap. No way man, the louder and crazier, the better.

"It's me, man, in all my handsomeness." Billy did a couple moon walk steps and bowed. He swiped at the powder around his nose, as his crystal blue eyes danced in his head.

"No shit, Mister Rocket! I have every one of your records. You want to hear me sing one. Name one, go ahead, name one," Max said.

"I wish I had time, but business calls. Maybe next time you're out this way we can jam."

"Yeah, I'll hold you to it, man. I love you, dude."

"I love you to, man. Peace." Billy threw a piece sign.

Max snatched out and pretended to put in his pocket.

"You too, man. Love ya back, dude."

Chapter 3

The cellphone shimmied across the nightstand with each annoying buzz. Jinx Baily slapped at the irritating sound, knocked the phone to the floor and groaned. Rainy day light leaking through the blinds soaked the room in gloom. To a fly on the wall it would be assumed the room had been tossed by narc's looking for the motherlode cache of drugs. To the owner, the room was in its natural state. Total disarray. Bagged dry cleaning hung from door jams, a laundry basket with clean laundry was by the bathroom door. A second laundry basket stationed in a corner acted as a hoop for dirty clothes. It was evident that Jinx was a bad shot, wads of clothing circled the basket. A choking smell of cigarette smoke, strong whiskey, stale greasy takeout food, and neglect filled the stagnant air in the room.

Jinx Bailey was an alcoholic. He couldn't stop drinking even if he wanted to, and he didn't want to. He drank every day, all day, but never seemed to be drunk. He didn't slur his words when in the courtroom, or while spending his free time in the Sand Bar with friends. True, he was a bottom feeding mouthpiece that worked the courthouse hallways like an alley rat works a dumpster, but it covered his rent and bar tab and what little food he ate. It wasn't always that way, at one time he was somebody, but that was all history. He was in Key West now and that was good enough.

Bailey swung his legs over the edge of the bed and sat up, pulled a pint bottle of hooch out of the nightstand drawer, splashed a water glass half full, and tossed it down. An instant later, he went into a hacking coughing fit that shook his body, rolling him forward in a breath-catching wheeze. He pulled a corner of the sheet up to his mouth as he fought to breath around the deep gasping. The spell lasted another moment then subsided. He let the sheet drop without looking at it, he knew there would be blotches of blood on it. The hacking spells were coming more often, and the blood increasing. He ignored it and stood using the night stand for support. He wobbled and sat back down, leaned forward and retrieved the phone. He recognized the Sand Bar number on the screen and hit the button.

"Jinx? Thank god. I need you to meet me at the sheriff's office, Jack's being held on a murder charge . . ."

"Whoa, slowdown, Coco. You're not making any sense," he said, as he splashed another drink into the glass.

"Okay, okay, let me start over. Dave Barnes, the deputy, stopped by after his shift to tell me that Sheriff Polk is holding Jack on a murder charge. He said that

Polk's acting like the case is closed on the murder based on Jack's history . . ."

"What history? Jack doesn't have a history." Jinx fired up a butt from the ashtray.

"That's what I said. Dave agreed, he didn't come right out and say it, but I know he believes Polk is still trying to pin Jack for the shooting of his deputy a few months back."

"This smells of Polk. He hates him, Coco. Give me twenty minutes and I'll meet you at the bar."

"I'll give you ten minutes and I'll be there to pick you up. Max is here, he'll drive us over."

The ride over to the sheriff's office was slow going, the rain was a steady drumming on the roof of the van. Max had the air conditioner on full blast, but the windows still fogged up.

"When are you going to spring for a Freon refill on this damn crate, Max? You need to consider the comfort of your customers," Jinx said, wiping his brow with a soiled kerchief.

"When are you going to be Attorney General?" Max shot back, as he peered out the foggy windshield. "Let me tell you something, Key West ain't the money capital of the world you know. I charge a few bucks to take a fare from point A to point B for a couple of dollars and they bitch about it. My life is in constant danger out here. What am I going to say if some palooka sticks a knife in my throat and wants my money? I'll tell you what I'll say . . . take it. It ain't worth it out here. I need to keep my expenses down, know what I mean?"

"Watch the road," Coco said, as she wiped the windshield.

"Hey, did I tell you guys who I yakked with this morning?" Max was suddenly animated bouncing to a tune only he could hear.

"I have a feeling you're going to tell us, even if we say we don't care," Jinx said.

"Billy Rocket, that's who. Frigging Billy Rocket!"

"Who?"

"Screw you, Jinx. The Rocket Man is the world's greatest guitar player that ever lived, and that includes Hendrix. Jimi was a punk compared to Rocket."

"Whatever," Jinx said. "All that heavy metal stuff is for societies losers, Max. It's all a bunch of psycho-babble, you can't make heads or tails out of the lyrics."

"That makes my point, Counselor. See what I must contend with, Coco? Some suit is talking about something he knows nothing about. I'll bet he doesn't even know who the drummer is for Bon Jovi."

"Watch the road, Max," Coco repeated.

Once inside the sheriff's annex, they had to be buzzed in to gain access to the desk sergeant.

"We are here to see Sheriff Polk, please," Jinx said, with authority.

"Ain't available," the officer answered.

"Then I would like to see my client, Jack Marsh."

"Ain't available."

"Then I would like to see the arresting officer."

"Ain't here."

Jinx wanted to reach across the desk and slap the insolent bastard, but he controlled his feelings.

"I would like to see the charges filed against my client."

"Ain't ready yet," the man sneered.

"Look, young man, do you realize who you are talking to?"

"Yeah, I know who you are, now scram," he said, condescendingly. "Be over at the courthouse at 2100. Your boy will be arraigned at that time."

Jinx felt a momentary twitch of shame then held himself erect.

"Very well then. Night court it is. Thank you for your help, Sergeant."

"I ain't a sergeant, I'm a deputy. The sergeant took a sick day. He and his old lady are having a beef of some kind. Ask me, he should dump her."

"I didn't ask you, and I'm sure the sergeant would resent you telling people about his personal problems."

The deputy pointed to the door, "Go!"

Max made it a point to push the door open wide enough that the latch caught. Slanting rain poured into the entry way.

"Hey, ya smart ass, close that door," the deputy yelled.

Max held both hands over his head, flipping him off,

"Eat a big one, ya jerk," Max yelled back, laughing.

Back in the cab, Max turned for instructions.

"Where to, folks? We got time to kill before we can spring Jackie."

"We need to get over to the *Queen*. I want to tell Bull what's going on. He needs to know about Sheila, too. They had sort of a friendship going. When he hears that Lamont reported back to me that little Mikey is missing he's going to go crazy. He loves that boy like his own." Coco said.

Chapter 4

Max pulled into the crushed coral lot that Island Salvage shared with The Raw Bar, a popular eatery and drinking hole favored by the locals. The stenciled sign hanging over the wood frame shack read, *'Island Salvage'*. The sub-line proclaimed, *'We Drag & Dive the Deep.'* Just below that boastful mission statement was *'Owner, Jack Marsh, Skipper, Chief Bull Drummond.'*

The shack was filled with dive gear, tackle, tanks, and a hundred other nautical gadgets. Most of the time, Bull didn't even bother unlocking the front door to the place, he spent his time in the back on the *Island Queen*. In fact, he seldom left the salvage boat except for supplies or to sign-in and suit-out tourists that paid for a day out on the water. When business was slow, Bull would get the word out around the hotels and dive shops that the *Queen* was available for day trips out to the Dry Tortugas or the Marquesas Keys.

"Bull, you aboard?" Max called out, as he hopped over the gunwale.

"I'm in the engine room, come on aboard." Bull's voice was deep and raspy from thirty years of Navy watch coffee. There wasn't an ocean he hadn't sailed on or a port where he wasn't known. His arms and torso were faded blotches of women's names he had long forgotten.

"Come on up, Bull. I need to talk to you," Coco called out, dreading what she had to do next.

"Right up, grab a cup of joe," came the reply.

Coco spotted Jinx disappear into the Raw Bar across the parking lot, and frowned. She liked him and worried that someday he would be found in an alley dead, or just disappear never to be seen again.

"What's up, Beautiful? You finally change your mind about working in a gin joint with me working your gorgeous butt out the backdoor?"

Bull was a big barrel-chested man with huge arms, hands to match, and a shaved head. He hugged Coco tight, helping himself to one of her buns.

"One of these days, Bull, I'm going to say yes and the first thing I'll do is cut your little sailor off."

"Ouch!" Bull let go in mock fear.

They both laughed at their basic greeting banter.

"What brings you and Wylie Coyote out here. Who's watching the bar" Bull asked.

"Watch your mouth, ya deck ape," Max shot back.

Coco lost it, she began to cry. She wrapped her arms around Bull's neck, and let it pour out, "Sheila's dead, Bull. They found her in the mangroves this morning. They are accusing Jack of murdering her . . . Lil' Mikey's missing. I don't know what to do . . ."

"What! Dead? I don't believe it. We were together just a couple of days ago. Who did it, where's Mikey?" Bull's mind was in shock and his heart was beating out of his chest. He loved Sheila like a man would love a daughter if he had one, and loved her child as a father would love a grandson.

"I don't know where he is. He's not at home or school. Lamont is out looking for him now."

"What's the sheriff saying? Do they know who did it, any leads . . ."

"Polk is accusing Jack of murder. He's going to be arraigned tonight at nine."

"That's crazy. Jack wouldn't kill her. Polk's got a grudge against Jack, but I didn't think he would pull a stunt like this. Have you contacted Jinx?"

"Yes, he's here with us. He ducked into the Raw Bar for . . . a take-out."

"Take-out my ass. Max, go grab him, we need him sober."

At 8:00 pm, Jinx led his little band of supporters into the wing of the sheriff's office that served as a venue for night court. Arrests made throughout the day up and down Monroe County were transported to the facility for arraignment. Because of limited space in the county jail, most offenders were released on their own recognizance. Marital disputes, public drunkenness, drug related offenses, petty theft, and the odd felony were all routine in the Keys and were usually released to a relative or to their lawyers if they had one.

Judge Marjorie Powers, known as Mad Madge for her propensity to blink rapidly and shake little fistlets as she ruled against those brought before her, entered promptly at 2100 hours.

"All rise," the bailiff boomed.

She took her time seating herself. Once seated, she gazed out across the crowded room of relatives, victims, lawyers, and posers, all from up and down the Keys social strata. Out of her court robes, she was often referred to as almost pretty but for a slight flaw in her smile that appeared as a grimace giving her the look of being pissed off all the time. In her robes, she worked the smile to her advantage bringing hesitation to those that fell under her hammer.

"Let's get this circus started," she hammered. "Be seated, talking, smoking, cell phones, crying, or any other disturbance will not be tolerated. We have many cases tonight and I have a sick dog at home, so keep quiet until you are outside."

It was after midnight before Jack shuffled into the courtroom wearing an orange jumper with hands and feet shackled, a deputy on either side. Coco gasped at Jack's black and blue swollen eyes. He looked over at her and shot a lopsided grin her way. A front tooth was missing.

"Jinx, what have they done to him?"

"Shhh, sit tight, we'll find out soon enough," he whispered back.

Judge Powers silently read the charges and then looked at Jack. His injuries were fresh, one cut under his eye was seeping blood.

"Bailiff, wipe the prisoner's face. I won't have ambulatory arrestee's in my courtroom. Because of the seriousness of the charges, I will allow the prosecutor to go forward. But make note, in the future, prisoners are not to be brought before me if they are visibly injured."

"Object, Your Honor," Jinx shouted, as he joined Jack at the defendant table. "My client is injured. Injuries he didn't have before he was brought into custody. I demand that Mister Marsh be released into my custody immediately, so I can see that he gets treatment."

"Overruled." Mad Madge said. "Proceed."

"Your Honor, we have Mister Marsh charged with the capital crime of murder, resisting arrest, and attempted escape from custody. Prosecution asks that the, uh . . . suspect be held without bond until a court date is set."

Judge Powers looked suspiciously at the prosecuting attorney, knowing he was new at the job and was trying to make a name for himself. On the other hand, she knew Jack Marsh as a solid citizen of Key West, except for rumored criminal activities offshore but unproveable. She didn't care what he did outside the continental U.S. Her jurisdiction covered the Keys.

"I've read the preliminary report submitted by the sheriff and agree that the charges are very serious, but in light of Mister Marsh's outstanding reputation in the community, I don't think it will . . ."

"Your Honor, I must insist that he be held," Sheriff Polk demanded, from the prosecutors table.

Mad Madge pounded the gavel loudly, "Sit down and shut up, Sheriff Polk. I'm in charge in here and I say who talks and who doesn't. One more outburst like that and I'll have the bailiff remove you from my courtroom."

"Yes, Your Honor, I apologize. It's just that his crime is so heinous that he should not be freed to roam our county. That poor girl was brutally . . ."

"Silence! This man is not on trial. Keep your mouth shut, Polk."

"Your Honor, my client is not a murderer. That poor woman was a valued employee and friend to Mister Marsh. He treated her and her son like a daughter and grandson. Mister Marsh couldn't hurt a no-see-em . . ."

"Stow the sob story, Mister Bailey. It's late and I'm not in the mood for your blathering."

"Blathering," Jinx said, indignantly. "Your Honor, I am an officer of the court . . ."

"Jinx, sit down and shut up." Madge read the charge sheet again and sat thinking.

"Sheriff Polk. Is it true that the charged resisted arrest?"

"Yes, Your Honor, it is."

"Is it true that he attempted to escape custody from the county facility?"

"Yes, Your Honor, it is."

"Bail denied." The hammer fell.

The court room exploded in a frenzy. Bull charged toward Sheriff Polk with hands outstretched and murder in his eyes, screaming, "You lying son of a bitch." A deputy grabbed him in a headlock and they went down in a flurry of fists.

Jack was hustled out of the courtroom by the two deputies with hatred in their eyes, Coco went for the bench, horrified at the injustice that had just occurred.

Jinx was on his feet shaking a fist, "Your Honor, this is a travesty of justice. How could you do this to a citizen of Mister Marsh's caliber?"

"Watch it, counselor, or you'll find yourself in a cell along with your client."

"Madge, it's not right and you know it," Jinx said, disgustedly to the one person in his life that really meant anything to him.

"Watch how you address me, Counselor. This is a court of law." Mad Madge spun around and disappeared through the door a deputy was holding open for her.

The mood in the Sand Bar was somber. Jack was in a cell charged with murder. Bull was somewhere in lock-up for fighting with an officer. Sheila was dead. Little Mikey was missing, and it was still pouring rain. A tropical low sat over the lower Keys and was forecast to stay there for a few days. It was three in the morning and the bar was shuttered, the only light was leaking from under the kitchen door and a neon beer sign that hung over the small stage blinking erratically.

"We all need a good night's sleep," Lamont said, over a wide yawn. "Some of us have to work for a living around here."

"I might stay closed for a couple of days in honor of Sheila, I don't know yet," Coco said.

"That will give us time to find Mikey, hopefully. My God, if something happened to that child, I'll just die," she whispered in tears.

"We're doing everything we can to get the word out around town to find him," Renée, one of the Sand Bar waitresses said. "Cookie is working old town talking to folks, Scarlet is riding her scooter around Searstown and Key West Bight with no luck and Blue hung around the school all afternoon and evening with no Mikey."

"Where's Blue now?" Coco asked. "He should be at the halfway house in bed or he's going back to prison for sure."

Jack often had parolees signed over to him as a sponsor, giving them jobs around the Sand Bar or on the *Island Queen* as deckhands while they worked off their time in a halfway house before being released out to the world. Everyone needs a second chance, he was fond of saying. Lamont had been with him for several years after spending time in Florida's prison system for seven years convicted of murder. He killed his mother's boyfriend for beating on her. Blue, whose real name was Mathew Turner but called Blue because of his bright crystal blue eyes, was another criminal Jack was sponsoring. Blue had spent three years in Florida's Raiford Prison for murder in the commission of a robbery. Raiford was a tough place, it was home to Florida's death row and execution chamber. He swore that his girlfriend-accomplice killed the liquor store clerk while he was in the car asleep the whole time. The jury, reluctantly, found him guilty and the judge went light on him with a ten-year bounce.

"I dropped him off earlier myself," Lamont said. "He was sure upset about Sheila. He told me that every time he had something going with a girl something happened to her. Nothing ever seemed to work out for him."

"What? He didn't have anything going with her, if she had anything going with anyone it was with Bull," Renée said, as she shook her long blonde locks.

Coco was disturbed about this turn of events.

"What else did he say, Lamont?"

"Nothing much. He said they had gone out a couple of times, but nothing ever came of it. He said it was too bad that she had a kid, that could be a deal breaker for him because he couldn't see himself as a daddy to someone else's child. He sounded mad when he was talking about Mikey. I even asked him why he was so upset, and he just shrugged it off and went inside to check in."

Coco didn't comment, she filed that tidbit of information away just as she did so many other scraps of information that came her way. In her line of work, it could be of use someday, one never knew.

"Okay, let's shut it down and get some rest. We'll stay closed tomorrow, but I want us to all meet here at noon to see what is happening regarding Mikey and Bull." Coco was beat, she had been on her feet since six the previous morning. A nice hot shower and a few hours of uninterrupted sleep would do her wonders.

"I'm for that, I could sleep a month," Lamont yawned. "Hey, where's Jinx? He was with us in Max's taxi. What up with that?"

"Speak correctly, Lamont, you're not in the 'hood' any longer," Coco admonished. "He was going over to talk some reason into Judge Powers to release Jack."

"Lots of luck with that. She has a bad rap inside all of Florida's prison units, there are boys inside doing crazy time that ain't right because of that old bitch . . ."

"Watch your mouth, boy," Coco drew a hand back to slap him. "You know I don't tolerate nasty language from anyone working here."

"Aw, Miss Coco that ain't nasty, it ain't clean, but it ain't dirty neither. It's one of them 'oxicompository' words. People use it all the time. Know what I'm sayin'?"

"Lord, spare me," Coco said, rolling her eyes.

Chapter 5

Jack ached. It had been a long time since he had taken a licking like the one he got from the deputies when they brought him in. Payback was going to be a bitch, all three of the men that did the beatdown were frequent visitors to the Sand Bar kitchen's backdoor looking for the obligatory burger or grouper sandwich. Jack never begrudged giving the lawmen free food, it was goodwill well spent, he knew they would keep an eye on his place because of this simple gesture. He fed the city cops in Key West and the county deputies alike when they came knocking. It was done in every city and town in the country, scratch their back, they scratch yours, but after tonight all bets were off.

Jack ran his fingers over his face tenderly, feeling the damage. A piece of polished stainless steel hung over the washbasin in the cell that served as a mirror, but it had so many initials and sorrowful laments of remorse and innocence scratched into it he couldn't make out the damage done to him. Oh well, it was probably better to think of himself as he looked just a few hours ago. He laughed but just as quick stopped from the pain it caused. So much for the Don Johnson look, he thought. He didn't like being compared to him anyway. The guy was a phony, an actor. He never saw the similarities and thought of himself as just an old jarhead with a square mug, white bright teeth, a ready smile, light brown hair, and sparkling blue eyes. Even in his early forties, he still worked out as often as he could, kept his weight at a constant two-hundred, and took on all comers in the boxing ring. Don Johnson? Never heard of her.

"Gimme a smoke," his cell mate spoke for the first time from the upper bunk.

Jack ignored the man. He didn't plan on being in jail long enough to become buddy-buddy with anyone.

"You heard me, I said gimme a smoke," the voice demand again.

Jack stood and turned facing the prone man. In a flash he grabbed the man's ear and twisted.

"I'm really not in the mood to play games with you, punk. You want to come down from there and snap ass holes, then come on down, otherwise shut the fuck up." Jack tugged hard on the ear then let go.

"Damn dude. What the fuck? You almost tore my ear off. I wasn't looking for trouble," the cellmate said, in a much-changed whiney voice. "I'm just trying to get by, dude. You been in here as long as me you have to set the margins, lines in the sand, shit like that, real quick. Take it from me, I know. Bastards' pin you to the floor and do ya like animals."

"Shut up." Jack's head ached, not some sissy headache but a hammer pounding an anvil ache. He was sure his nose was broken by the way it moved when he tried to clear it. A little light seeped into his right eye, but the left was lights out. He ran his tongue over where his right front tooth had been earlier in the day and flinched. The exposed nerve snapped like a whip shooting pain up to the anvil in his head. He was exhausted, he was sick to his stomach and the pain from his bruised body simmered. He wanted to lay down and sleep. He stood and faced his bunk buddy again.

"Hey, boy-toy, I'm going to catch some sleep. If I even hear your feet touch the deck I'm going to break a leg off and beat you with it. Understood?"

"Uh . . . yeah . . . uh . . . I mean, yes sir . . . sir, no trouble from me that's for sure."

"Good, you behave I'll let you climb down from your bunk in a while."

"Peace, bro."

Jack laid back gently on the steel bunk, wiggled a couple of times, and began to drift almost immediately. What kind of a fix was he in now, how was it going to turn out . . .

'People came to the Keys for many reasons, some to party, some on the run from the law, others to hide from what they left behind on the mainland, wives, lovers, abusive partners, you name it. Jack could tell in an instant which category a person fell into, he was a master at it. Ten years earlier he had hit town with a few bucks, looking over his shoulder to see who was following him, and ahead for opportunities. Jack and Key West were made for each other, they were alike, brothers from different mothers as they said back in L.A. He worked hard as a bartender for a joint on Duval seven night a week. In the daylight hours he worked as a dive boat skipper making runs out to the Tortugas every day with a boatload of vacationing tourists. He worked and watched, kept his mouth shut and his ears open, learning the game of survival in a place that produced nothing, built nothing, and offered nothing but booze and the lie of tropical splendor.

The first year was work and no play, he learned quickly to not trust everything he heard, and not to believe everything he saw. He understood fast that everyone was working a scam or running a score. The targets were usually the tourists, but not always. Sometimes the action spilled over the line sucking in *locals. When that happened justice was swift and sometimes deadly. It was not uncommon for someone to just go missing.*

"Whatever happened to what's his face?" someone would ask.

"Him? I think he went down island, maybe Jamaica."

"The bastard owes me money."

"Good luck with that."

Yeah, Jack watched and learned. The owner of the bar found out he was dying of cancer and thought a quart of Cuervo a day would cure it. It didn't. Jack bought the place from the man's estate on a loan from the Key West National. He refurbished and updated the place, and reopened as Sand Bar. He promoted the bar as the go to place for booze and gumbo. The waitresses were decked out as Island Girls each with a hibiscus in her hair, a halter top, and a sarong brief with a lot of thigh showing. The tourists loved it. Within a year his Sand Bar was the most popular watering hole on Duval Street. With that popularity came opportunities, some good some bad, then others very bad or very good . . . and very dangerous.'

"Wake up, Marsh. You're going for a ride."

Jack jerked upright from a restless slumber. Hands pulled him to his feet, swung him around and had the shackles locked before he was even awake.

"What the hell?" He was confused for a moment and then the pain hit. A million wasp stings exploded across his face as one of the deputies laid a roundhouse on him.

"That's a good morning kiss from the sheriff, Marsh," the jailer laughed.

Jack staggered and fell, warm blood and snot from his broken nose and cut mouth ran down his chin. He shook his head again attempting to clear it. He was yanked to his feet again and bunny hopped out of the cell and down the hallway.

Outside, a deputy waited in his car with the motor running, the unit's wipers slapping at the downpour. Jack was shoved into the backseat and the door slammed behind him. A moment later the passenger side door opened, and the sheriff slid in. Sheriff Polk sat for a moment in thought, water dripped from the brim of his short-brimmed Stetson.

"Jack, you fucked up for the last time," he began. "You know, and I know you killed Deputy Kilpatrick. Fuck what the jury said. I was there, I watched Kilpatrick run into that building, and then you ran out. You shot Kilpatrick just as sure as I'm sitting here in this rain. I'll tell you straight up though, I won't lie to you, you're going to pay for it."

"Fuck you, Polk." Jack winced with pain, as he spoke. "You've crossed the line, Sheriff. Just as soon as I get out of here, I'm getting Bill Price from The FBI on your ass." It sounded like *ath* coming from his broken mouth.

Polk laughed, and slapped his knee, "Jack, you remember the Marines' Red Line Brig over in Corpus Christi? Where they sent the bad fellas to get reeducated and rehabilitated from their criminal ways? Some of them boys went in and never came out, when they did come out, they were in body bags out the backdoor, shipped home to momma."

Jack was having a hard time following Polk. He knew the Red Line Brig very well, He spent nine months there as a prisoner chaser after he came back from Iraq. Without a doubt, the prisoner abuse and harassment that went on inside those walls and huts was legend. It was reserved for hardcore criminals that were marking time waiting to be transferred to Leavenworth or the Supermax prison facility in Colorado to never see daylight again. The entire compound was controlled by red, yellow and green painted lines. There were no barred doors or hallways. If a prisoner was running from point A to point B, he was allowed on the Green line. Yellow, if told to stop by a guard. Red line for physical punishment. God help the inmate that stepped across the redline, he would be beaten unconscious and left there as an example to the other inmates. Often an inmate would be pulled across the red line and beaten just for the hell of it. Jack hated the duty and still thought that some of the guards were worse criminals than the inmates.

"What are you talking about, Polk? Jinx made my bail, right?"

Polk turned, his face ugly with hate, "Afraid not, Marsh. There's not going to be any bail for you, as a matter of fact you may never see the light of day again where you're going."

"What are you talking about?"

"You remember Major Cotton from your old duty station in Corpus?"

"What does Cotton have to do with anything?"

"Cotton's a friend of mine, he's Warden for FDC's Everglades Correctional Institution now. He quit the Corps when things got a little hot for him, FDC snapped him up. They needed a good man to shape up the Everglades unit and love the results to date. Since we're so tight on space down here, he's agreed to take you in for a while. He's expecting you, Marsh. It will be like old home week for the two of you." He laughed, as he got out of the patrol unit, then stuck his head back in, "Nice knowing you, Jack. I hear the Everglades are a bitch this time of year what with all those gators and snakes."

"Hey, wait a minute. Polk, you can't do this. What the hell are you pulling, you bastard!"

Sheriff Polk pulled the slicker collar up tight against the rain, as he watched the patrol unit pull out of the lot. Jack Marsh was twisted around in the seat glaring at the sheriff. Their eyes were locked in hate, and then the rain swallowed them up.

Chapter 6

The Key West Cemetery was a gloomy place on sunny days, and downright spooky on rainy days. The quarter square mile was home for over a hundred thousand of the dearly departed starting back in 1847 to present day. Those that dealt in such things would tell you that there was an ever-growing population in their little plot for the dead and there wasn't any end in sight for the need. Anyone with a pocket calculator could quickly tell you that the math didn't work as for space divided by occupancy. That same calculator could tell one that the elevation of the cemetery compared to sea level grew once every fifty years. In layman's terms, the city fathers knowing that older generations had died off or moved on simply removed the above ground sarcophagi and vaults, laid down a few feet of fresh sod and *BINGO,* they were back in business. Sure, old Conch family plots were never touched. They were kept as a token of respect to those that had made their fortunes off the less prosperous of the city's dwellers. Transients unlucky enough to croak in Key West were quietly cremated and tossed in the dumpster behind the hospital out on Stock Island.

Little Mikey Pollack didn't know and didn't care about any of the shenanigans of the city fathers, he was scared shitless. He was cold, hungry, wet, and afraid. Afraid probably wasn't descriptive enough, he was fucking terrified. He had taken up residence in the Beatrice and Wendell Weaver vault in the center of the cemetery, mainly because the rusty old wrought iron gate was partially open, and he could squeeze through. The tile floor inside was covered with grime, old food wrappers, a pair of stinky boxer shorts, cigarette butts, used condoms, and corners piled with accumulated filth, but it was sanctuary from the monster man who hurt his mother. He knew if the man found him he would rape him, too, and then choke him to death.

Mikey began to cry, he knew his mother was hurt and maybe worse. The memory of her being carried into the mangroves still haunted him. He should have done something, but he didn't know what. If he was older and bigger he would have done something serious. Six and a half was no match against a full-grown man. But for as long as he lived he would remember everything that happened . . . forever.

"'Get your shit together, little man, we're going for a ride," the man had said, as he pulled his mom across the cement floor.

Mikey started to cry watching his mother fight against the man. When she arrived home, she and he were laughing and drinking.

"Mikey get your jammies on and curl up on the couch, mommy will be out in a few minutes then you can hop in bed," Sheila had said.

Less than fifteen minutes later, the bedroom door flew open and the man began to yell. Sheila had a bloody nose, little droplets of blood splattered her bare chest each time the man slapped her.

"You leave my mom alone, you dog butt," Mikey yelled and kicked the man in the calf.

"You little shit." A hand came out of nowhere and slapped Mikey off his feet. "Shut up and do as I say. I've got something special for you and your mom, now git."

The man hit his mother with his fist and she went limp and fell to the floor. He picked her up and yelled to Mikey,

"Let's go, runt. Your momma's going to have some fun and then it'll be your turn."

That slap was the worse pain he had ever experienced except for the time Duncan Yeager chunked a rock off the back of his head when he was little and they lived in Houston. He got eight stitches for that and still had the scar to prove it. He wondered if he would need stitches for the slap, he thought, as he fingered his face for anything out of line or wet with his blood.

Mikey didn't know where they were, the car just seemed to go on and on forever. He recognized Searstown, then the Kmart where they shopped. He saw the Holiday Inn sign and when the car turned left then drove over the bridge he knew they were going towards Miami. But then the man turned left and drove for a couple of minutes then turned off onto a crushed coral road. The whole time while driving his mother lay slumped over in the front seat and the man whistled and laughed. Mikey was beginning to think this may turn out all right after all, the man seemed happy enough.

The man turned off the motor and the lights. He sat looking around like he was watching for a friend to show up. After a couple of minutes, he got out and walked around to the passenger side and opened the back door.

"I'm going to tell you this one time and you better listen up." He flashed out a shucking knife and waved it in front of Mikey's face. "You let out any screams and I'll cut your little jalapeno off."

Mikey was frozen in fear, there was no doubt that he would cut his wiener off. He knew if that happened he would never be able to pee again.

"Yes, su . . . su . . . sir," he stuttered.

The man pulled his mother out of the car by the arm and lifted her on to the hood. Mikey watched as he cut his mom's panties off with the shucking knife. He craned his neck to see over the front seat but couldn't tell what was going on. Scared, but curious, he scooted out of the car and disappeared in the shadows of an old gumbo-limbo tree to watch. His mind couldn't comprehend what the man was doing but knew enough to know he would catch hell if his mom knew he was watching. He had spied on her before when she would bring boyfriends home to sleepover.

Sheila was unconscious and didn't know when the shucking knife sank deep into her throat then pulled across to the other side. Her head hung at a strange angle. She didn't feel the blade either when it entered her vagina and ripped upwards through the pubic bone then downward threw the perineum into her rectum. She didn't know.

    Mikey watched as the man went limp for a moment then pull his pants up. He saw the man's wiener and gulped, it was huge and swollen. I bet that hurts, he thought. He faded deeper into the shadows and watched the man lift his mom up and throw her over his shoulder. He stifled a sob when he saw her head bounce crazily as she was carried into the mangroves. Somehow, he knew he was next, without even being aware of it he began to run as fast as he could away from the monster that he knew was coming for him next.'

As he remembered, Mikey sobbed in heart wrenching pain, his little body shuddered. He was in deep trouble but didn't know what to do. He couldn't go to school; Miss Brady would be mad at him for missing two days of lessons and besides his clothes were all dirty and smelled like dead people. He pulled his legs up tight to his chest and began to rock back and forth, was hungry and scared and missed his mom.

Chapter 7

The falling rain was slowed by the double canopy of trees, vines and tropical vegetation but still managed to roll down Chief Bull Drummonds neck around his slicker as he watched the sheriff's forensic team work the murder scene around where Sheila's body had been found. The sheriff had thrown him in the drunk tank after the courtroom scuffle then without a word popped him out at five in the morning along with the other vagrants and drunks. This wasn't a kindness on the sheriff's part, it was because it saved the county money by not having to feed the men breakfast.

Bull had returned to the *Island Queen* for quick shower, shave, and clean clothes followed by a pot of strong coffee. He knew Jack was in deep trouble but wasn't sure what Sheriff Polk's game was. And what about Judge Powers? She was Jinx's lady friend and yet, she acted like that judge on television, the one with the wiseass answers to everything. What the hell was going on? He could smell trouble, but he had no doubt that he would put it all together as time went by. His years of time spent in the blue water navy had taught him to solve a problem by first understanding what the problem was. He knew it started with Sheila being murdered so he decided to go out and see where the crime had been committed.

There really wasn't much left to see because of the rain.

"What about clothing, shoes maybe? She always wore little gold hoop earrings I gave her for her birthday," Bull asked.

"I said you could watch, not ask questions, Bull." Deputy Anderson liked Bull, they were both Navy vets and shared sea stories out at the Boca Chica Staff NCO club. "Everything that is important is gone. I'm just taking a closer look to see to see if we missed anything. But this damn rain has washed everything away."

"It's forecast to keep pouring for another couple of days," Bull threw in, craning his neck to see what he could see. "When's the autopsy going to be finished?"

Anderson shot a look, and said, "You don't need to worry about that, Bull, it's just going to make you crazy. Just suck it up that Sheila is gone. How she went will be worked out by the coroner. All in due time, Master Chief." He didn't want to say anything about the deceased having been dead before she was raped and mutilated. Probable cause of death was a blow to the head. The lack of blood flow from the savage cut to the throat and vaginal area implied that the heart had stopped pumping resulting in minimal blood loss. His friend didn't need to know those kinds of details.

Satisfied that nothing new was going to be found, the two men trudged out of the knee deep fetid water and made their way back to their vehicles. Bull was about to thank Anderson for letting him onto the crime scene when he saw a sheriff unit driving by heading towards Highway 1.

"Hey, that's Jack in the back of that unit," Bull said, swinging his head to Anderson then back to the patrol car as it moved away. "What's up with that? Where are they taking him?"

"Beats me, maybe over to the Navy Hospital to sew him up." Anderson scratched his head.

"Nah, too early, those squid doctors don't even show up until nine or ten."

Alarm buzzers were going off in Chief's brain. Something wasn't right. Three giant steps got him to his pickup then he was inside firing it up.

"Thanks, Ed. I'll be in touch." Bull hit the pedal and the twin cab heavy duty pickup fishtailed onto the asphalt street.

Traffic on Highway 1 was light going in both directions as Bull maintained a steady 60mph a quarter mile behind the deputy's unit. He was having a tough time trying to understand where they were taking Jack. He should be in a cell back on Stock Island, but for some reason he was being taken north, maybe to the Marathon station.

He hit speed dial for Coco, "It's me," he said, as soon as he heard her answer. "Jack's in the back-seat of a sheriff's car heading north. I don't know what Polk is up to, but you better get Jinx on it."

"Where are you now?" She asked, as she swung out of bed.

"We're blowing through Big Pine, I think they must be taking him to the Marathon facility to hold him there. I'll hit you back as soon as I know more." He clicked off and tossed his phone on the passenger seat.

The deputy kept his speed steady through Bahia Honda, across the seven-mile bridge and into Marathon. He became alarmed when they past Fisherman's Hospital and then Marathon Airport.

"What the hell is going on?" He said aloud to himself.

Traffic picked up south of Islamorada and stayed heavy through Key Largo. At Florida City the patrol car pulled off onto the crushed coral lot in front of the Last Chance Bar and Package Store and cut the motor. Bull drove past and pulled into a gas station and parked where he could see what the hell was happening. Five minutes later, a black SUV sped down the highway with blue and white lights twirling, pulled into the lot in a cloud of coral dust and threw on the breaks. Two husky uniformed men jumped out of the SUV, opened the deputy's back door and pulled Jack out. Without a word, they hopped him across the lot and shoved him into the backseat. Both men climbed in and sped away.

Bull hit the gas and followed, at the intersection he turned left and almost rear-ended the SUV. A school bus a few cars ahead was letting off a gaggle of kids and traffic was stopped in both directions. The bus moved on and the traffic started moving. When the cop car turned onto State Road 9336, he knew where they were taking Jack . . . the Everglades Correctional Institution. ECI had the rap of being the toughest work camp in the country, just behind Louisiana's Angola Prison. Both prisons are infamous for men going in and never getting out, the ones that did come out the front gate were changed men forever, physically and mentally damaged.

Coco picked up the call on the first ring, "Where are you, Bull?"

"I'm just outside Florida City watching two goons take Jack inside ECI," he said, frustrated that there was nothing he could do short of ramming his rig through the gate and grab Jack before he disappeared inside the prison.

"Oh, God, what more can happen . . ." Coco said.

Bull could hear fear in her voice. Coco never got rattled, never.

"Talk to me, Princess. What's wrong?"

"Renée didn't show up for our meeting. Max went by her place and pounded on the door, a neighbor said she hadn't seen her since yesterday. Something's going on, Bull, I don't understand."

"Stay put, I'm on my way."

Bull shot the front gate a last look, Jack had disappeared inside. He down shifted and popped the clutch. The engine whined in pain then caught traction and leaped forward.

"What the hell was going on?" he said again, slamming his fist on the steering wheel.

Chapter 8

The cold water from the hose hit Jack like a thousand needles that snapped his body into a curl on the shower floor. The force of the water skidded him across the cement deck into a corner. He tried to turn his back to the powerful firehose but failed. Caked scabby blood dissolved and ran down his face and torso in red watery rivulets. A cut above his eye opened and flowed freely.

"That's enough," shouted a man in a starched military-pressed uniform. "On your feet Marsh, we need to talk."

Major Cotton's voice, once heard, would never be forgotten. It was a mix of whiskey scarred vocal cords and two packs of cigarettes a day over a life time. Jack tried to obey, but slipped hitting his chin a painful whack. He managed to get on all fours when a tremendous blow to his midsection knocked the air out of him.

"I tell you to stand, you stand, boy!" Warden Cotton bellowed. "Stand him up, I ain't got all day."

Two burly men in short sleeved denim shirts grabbed him roughly and hauled him to his feet. Jack tried to straighten but the pain from the kick was still radiating out.

"Stand at attention, boy. Back straight, chin in, chest out, thumbs along the seams of your trousers. Oops, my bad, you aren't wearing trousers. Get used to it. Your days of playing pretty boy are over Marsh. I didn't like you when you were in the Corps with me and I don't like you now. In fact, I think I'm on the verge of hating you for killing that whore down in Key West. That's stuff is free Jackie boy, you don't need to kill for it. Hell, gals give it away these days."

"Fuck you. I didn't kill anyone . . ." A fist smashed into his mouth.

"You don't talk unless I say so, boy. You just pretend your back in San Diego in boot camp. You don't talk, you don't eat, you don't shit, you don't live unless I say so."

Jack had enough of this bastard and lunged for him. He swung a roundhouse that glanced off Warden Cottons chin. Big mistake. In an instant he was down on the deck in a blizzard of boots, fists, clubs, yelling and curses. Somewhere a couple of more men joined in the beat down. A mean glancing kick to the head mercifully knocked him out.

'Somewhere in his mind he was riding horseback across a field of boulders and rock. The poor horse was winded and faltering even though Jack was not even holding the reigns. He tried to sit up straight in the saddle but leaned left and right catching himself at the last minute. The horse stumbled and went down, Jack flew over the saddle horn and yelled in pain.'

He snapped awake as he bounced again hitting his head on the bed of the pickup. Where the hell was he? Maybe, it was hell. He hurt everywhere. He had the crap beat out of him on top of the beatdown by the sheriff's men sometime long ago and far away. He opened an eye and cringed. He was in the bed of a truck with two other men. One of the men was sitting on the side rail dressed in jeans and a short-sleeved shirt rolled tight over huge biceps. He had a streetsweeper shotgun in his hand and the stock on his hip. The man's skin was slick with sweat and shined brighter than ebony. The other man was naked and bleeding, Jack knew it was blood because his body was shiny and wet against the reddish-brown skin.

Jack closed his eyes and faked sleep letting his body bounce and roll with the rhythm of the truck. He studied the guard through a swollen eye. Shaved head, thick forehead, wide set nostrils and bulbous lips. His arms were huge from either weight lifting or throwing cars in his spare time, blue prison tats ran down to his knuckles. The man reeked of danger. Jack noticed that he wasn't wearing shoes, the soles were calloused pads of dirt and grime.

"Where we going?" Jack asked. It was difficult to talk, his mouth was swollen, a canine tooth was missing. He wasn't sure if his jaw was broken or not, but it sure hurt sending shock waves through his right eye.

He winced, cleared his throat, and croaked, "Where are we going?"

The huge man shifted his head and focused on Jack, "We goin' to hell, white boy."

"Where is hell? I thought I had already arrived."

Muscle man sniggered, "You been in heaven compared to where we goin'. Now, shut the fuck up, you ain't supposed to talk unless a boss man say so."

A shudder ran down Jack's spine followed by a terrible foreboding of what was to come.

"What's your name?" he asked.

"Don't make no difference what my name is. Knowing me ain't going to do anything fo' you 'cept get yo' ass whupped."

"My name is Jack Marsh. If somebody asks you, tell them you saw me, okay?"

"You name is Jack shit to me, honkey. Somebody ax, you tell them you seen me whipping yo' ass, now shut the fuck up 'for I blow that scrawny dick of yours off."

They bounced in silence down the crushed coral road pulling a smoke screen of dust behind them.

"What's the matter with him," Jack flicked his chin towards the black kid bouncing on the steel deck.

"You sure are nosey. The onliest thing wrong with him is that he's alive. He's going to wish he was dead when Boss Dalton gets his hands on his redbone ass. I 'specs next time we see this boy he'll be in the alligator stew along with some taters and roots."

Jack looked at the man curiously, and said, "Excuse me? Alligator stew?"

"Maybe even a few moccasins for flavoring," he laughed.

"What's that red band around your sleeve. Is it some kind of rank?"

"It a rank all right. It allow me to beat the shit out of anybody Boss Dalton say. Sometimes, when he ain't around, I beat 'em up anyway."

"Swell, I'll bet you were a cop before you came here."

"I wasn't no cop. I hate pigs. I kills 'em if I get the chance."

"A real live cop killer, huh?"

"White boy, get it through yo' head, we ain't nobody alive here. We all dead, we just ain't down yet."

The truck came to a stop. A couple of men wearing palmetto woven hats peered into the bed.

"New meat," one said, around a mouth full of rotted teeth.

The other, "Uh huh, white meat. Hope he iss tender as that Tommy boy. Now, that's one fine young'un."

"Watch what you say, that's Boss Dalton's bitch. He dust you up he catch you even thinking about touching that sweet thing."

"Get 'em out of that truck," a voice boomed.

"Yes, suh, Boss," Jack's guard answered.

The tailgate was dropped, and rough hands pulled the unconscious figure out letting him flop to the ground. A hand wrapped around Jack's ankle and pulled. Jack lashed out with a vicious kick.

"Get your fucking hands off me," he shouted.

He was ignored, his shoulders bounced off the bumper and then he was dragged across the crushed coral.

"Get up, boy!"

Jack stumbled then stood. His brain was screaming for him to just roll with it all, don't fight back, suck it up. The sun was hot on his naked body, he forced himself to breathe the thick humid air through his broken nose, but it was blocked with blood. He put a thumb next to his nostril and blew, the pain shot through his head like an ice pick, but it cleared the nasal passage, he repeated the other side.

"You must be Marsh. Major Cotton told me all about you, he said you killed a gal down in Key West then raped her. Is that so?"

Jack looked at the uniformed man standing on a porch shaded by palm frond thatch. Sweat ringed his armpits.

"I didn't kill anyone. I shouldn't be here. Polk is behind this . . ."

"Shut Up! I didn't say you could talk."

The man became a blur as he leaped from the porch. An explosion of fire erupted in Jack's groin. He fell to the ground screaming in agony, a million volts of pain shot out as he cupped himself.

"You need to learn, boy, if you're going to survive, you need to learn fast. Rule number one is you never talk to me unless I say you can. If I give you permission, which I probably won't, you will address me as Boss Dalton, nothing else, just Boss Dalton."

The knots of pain began to ease as Jack's vision cleared as he continued to take short breaths. What was happening was incomprehensible. His situation was in doubt for the first time in years. He fell back on instinct and training, situational awareness, focus on your surroundings, look for weak spots, escape, survival . . .

"Get on your knees, boy. Rule number two, anytime you're in front of me, I want you on your knees with your eyes looking down at mother earth," Boss Dalton said, as he circled Jack. "Looks like you're slow on the draw based on those puny gunshot scars."

Jack didn't know if he was being asked about the three scars on his back or if the asshole was just commenting, so he kept his mouth shut. He took the chance to move his eyes around the compound. His first impression was of photos he had seen of prisoner camps from the Vietnam war, elevated wire cages, palmetto frond huts, heat balls roiling out from a thatched hut carrying some noxious food smell with it. Open-air huts with camping cots lined up in rows. The cooking smells mixed with the odor of human waste brought bile to his mouth.

"This is the way that it goes down, boy. You will obey all orders given you by the trustees. The trustees wear red or yellow arm bands, red arm bands are camp trustees, yellow bands are work trustees. Either color has the authority to carry out any punishment for any infraction of my rules, and I have many, some I haven't even thought up yet. We get up at sunrise and we go to bed at sundown. While you are here, you will work every day whether you are sick, lame, or just lazy. I will feed you a morning meal and a night meal. Any food other than that you'll have to get yourself from the wild. Under no circumstances will you bring food in from the field. I don't ever want to catch you bringing in a little snake meat or frog, or anything else you may find while you are working." Boss Dalton was pacing back and forth as he recited his litany of camp rules. "If you think you will be sent back to *'Mainside'* for medical treatment because you drank some of this shit water you'll be working in, you're wrong. You get a case of monkey butt out here, it's tough shit," he laughed and slapped his leg at his humor.

"Another thing, don't think you'll be leaving anytime soon, Marsh. You're out here for a reason," he bragged.

"Yeah, what reason is that?"

A fist smashed into Jack's face knocking him to the dirt.

"I guess you wasn't listening when I ran through rule number one. Mister Toby, dust him up a bit then put him in number three, let the skeeters at him for a couple of days and we'll see if he's learned any manners."

"Yas, suh, Boss." The trustee that had accompanied Jack in the back of the pickup snapped out.

"Come on, honkey, get up." Toby kicked with a deeply callused foot. "We going to step over here behind the bushes for a few minutes, I'll introduce you to Black Tom."

Chapter 9

Max was sitting in his taxi-van listening to a self-help cd on *'Character and Strength Building',* thinking about all the tourists that visit Key West that throw their hard-earned money away on tee shirts and stick-on tattoos to make themselves look tough for a few days, then fly back home or go back aboard ship in a haze of sunshine and bags of island trinkets all made in China. The ladies with Mai Tai umbrellas stuck behind an ear or in their hair, and the guys with a rum buzz having lived and survived the notorious Duval crawl. For a few hours they had lived the 'island life' and now had bragging rights, 'Been there, Done that.'

'That Jackie was one smart cookie, seems like everything he touches turns to gold, some guys just have all the luck. Take Billy Rocket, for example. He was just a younger version of himself, but he's known all over the world, he could live anywhere he wanted. So why the hell was he living in the Keys? He should be out on the coast, or playing Vegas, what's up with that? It don't make sense, a guy like that. Yeah and what's up with all that cash that punk had in the briefcase, dropping a c-note on me like it was nothing? A c-note for Christ's sake. I know mutts in Riker's doing a deuce bounce for stealing a hundred dollars. Wish there was a way to get my hands on that briefcase, that kind of money I'm talking a whole

fleet of cabs. I would take over the cab business from those shmucks at Key West Cab, they cheat every customer that gets in one of theirs. And those Uber mutts, the fuck was that all about? No better than scabs crossing the picket line.

Yeah, I need to get a piece of that briefcase, or I'll be sitting here for the rest of my life not going anywhere. Why am I listening to this motivational stuff anyway? I'm a natural leader just like those rich guys up on the East Side, you don't think they made their millions by stealing it from somebody else? You gotta be crazy to think they made their money by being honest and actually worked for it. I need to make something of myself before I get too old. I'm dying down here in the Keys. I need to be back in the world.'

He turned the key and listened as the motor tried to turn over, it caught, and he gunned the engine.

'I'll take a spin out to Shark Key and suck up to Billy, this might just put me up there with Jackie. I'll show him I can be somebody, too.'

Traffic was thin on Truman even though it was midday. The local forecast was for rain for the next couple of days, the low was centered over Havana with Key West on the northern edge of it. They say it could turn into a named storm, but they always say that to stir up the locals to buy stuff they don't need. That guy from Atlanta shows up on the scene and the place goes crazy snapping up everything from sand bags to bottled water.

The thing that goes first is toilet paper. Like who's going to need paper if there isn't anything to eat, for Christ sakes.

He was sitting at the light listening to the wipers slap back and forth when something caught his attention over by the Chinaman's store, Lok Kwok Sock whatever. It was just a flash of a little kid ducking behind the back of the building.

'Hey, was that Mikey, Sheila's boy? I better check this out. Coco would kill me if I saw the kid and didn't do nothing to catch him.'

The light turned green after an eternity. He whipped the cab out in front of the oncoming cars, they exchanged a blast of horns and finger waving, and then he was clear, *'F-ing snowbirds, ain't got a clue how to drive, must be from Michigan.'*

He cut into the small delivery area behind the store and hit the brakes just as a pair of scrawny legs disappeared into the dumpster.

Max jumped out of the van yelling, "Mikey . . . Mikey. It's me, Maxie. I'm Coco's friend from where your mom works . . . I mean worked before she got . . . never mind."

Mikey tried to hide under flattened corrugated boxes, old produce and other garbage. He ignored the calls searching for anything edible. He came up with a pear and devoured it, core and all.

"Mikey, it's me Max Simms, Jack Marsh's best friend. Come here. I'll take you to see Jack and Coco."

"Go away, I hate you. You have bad breath. Momma says you're horny for all the ladies at the Sand Bar."

"Watch your mouth, you little bastard, I'm trying to help you here. Keep up that kind of talk, I'll just slam this frigging door down and let the rats eat you."

"I ain't scare of rats or you. My momma told me never to trust strangers. You might be the monster man that hurt my momma."

"Listen kid, your beginning to piss me off. I didn't hurt your mother and I'm not horny for all the ladies at the Sand Bar. She must have been thinking about Lamont or that Blue character."

"He killed my momma." Mikey began to sob.

"Who killed your momma, Mikey? You know who it is, did you see him yourself?"

"Yes, it was the man with blue eyes. I saw him hurt my momma, he hit her, and she fell down and went to sleep."

"Jeez kid, that's awful you seen all that. What happened then?"

"We went for a car ride and the monster man with blue eyes told me to stay in the car while he put my mom on the hood of the car." The flood gates opened, and Mikey began to cry and sob. "Then . . . then, he told me I was next if I got out of the car or yelled or anything. I was so scared I pooped my pants. Momma's going to spank me for pooping myself."

"Yeah, I know what she means, you ain't supposed to shit yourself, Mikey, but under the circumstances, we'll keep it to ourselves, okay?"

"Yes, sir. Will you help me? I'm so scared and I want to go home. Mrs. Turner is going to be mad at me, too, for missing school. She'll probably call momma again like when I kicked Johnny in the peanuts."

"Don't worry, all women get mad when a guy kicks another guy in the peanuts. I'm an expert at it. When I fought for the Golden Gloves in Brooklyn, I was a champ. Of course, that was a long time ago, so they probably threw away the record books by now, so you just have to take my word for it. They was going to send me to the Olympics but they chickened out, I was sent to juvie instead. Now, come on out. I'll take you home."

"You promise you won't hurt me?"

Mikey had pear pieces around his mouth, his face was dirty, and tear streaked, his eyes wet and swollen. Max had a moment of compassion then pushed it down deep. No way was he going to go soft over the kid. Next thing people would be talking about him being a softy.

"Come over here and I'll help you out, I ain't going to hurt you."

Max helped Mikey into the backseat and buckled him in, brushed at his short sleeved white dress shirt and straightened his bow tie then he circled the van got behind the wheel and speed dialed Coco.

"Max, get over here. Bull is on his way back from Florida City, he knows where Jack is." Coco sounded frantic which was very unusual from her normal demeaner of calmness under just about all circumstances.

"Yeah? While Bull was chasing rainbows, I was working the case of the missing kid. Thank God, my personal experience in law enforcement helped me solve the mystery. I not only have the kid, I know who murdered Sheila Pollack . . ."

Mikey let out a huge sob, and cried out. "My momma's dead. You said you were taking me to her."

"I didn't say I was taking you to her, I said I knew where she was, big difference, kid."

"Max! What's happening? You have Mikey?" Coco was beside herself with relief.

"Yeah, I got the kid and he's safe in my hands, but we have a Bluto among us. I know who the killer is."

"What are you talking about Max, speak plain English. You say some man named Bluto murdered Sheila?"

"Nah, Coco. Sheesh. Bluto, you know the guy that killed that Caesar guy played by Charles Laughton. Sometimes, I forget you was schooled in Haiti."

"Who killed her, Max? My God, we can turn him in to Sheriff Polk and get Jack freed."

"Uh-uh, no can do, Coco. I ain't exposing this boy to anymore drama, he's seen enough for such a tender age. He's lost his mother to a tragedy. I know how he feels, my own mother gave me up early in life too."

"Max, you're not making any sense. Bring Mikey here immediately or I'll have Bull come get him."

"No need to get hostile, I'm just saying I can't take him to the Sand Bar, that's where the murderer is."

"What!"

"Yep, the latest of Jack's ex-con's out on parole. Maybe this will teach him not to take in bad people."

"Max, need I remind you of your two-year stint in Rikers Correctional?"

"That's harsh, Coco, real harsh. I served my time honorably, even got my schooling inside."

"Max, I'm tired of playing word games, get your butt over here with Mikey, now!"

"I can't, Coco. Didn't you hear me? The killer is right there, probably within a few feet."

"Who is it, Max?"

"Blue."

"Blue? Why, that's impossible. He loved Sheila and Mikey."

"Coco, think about it, Blue never had a good word to say about the kid, he was just hot to get in Sheila's skivvies. I interrogated the kid and he told me the man had blue eyes, Duh! Put it together, Coco. Blue had access to Sheila, he had the hots for her, he goes over to score, they fight, he pops her one, the kid sees it all. Tell me I'm wrong."

"That's ridiculous, you are so far off from reality, Max. Blue knows if he does anything wrong his parole gets pulled and he's back in Raiford. I know for a fact that Lamont dropped him off at the halfway house the night Sheila was murdered."

"Hey, you don't want to see through the smoke and fog of war, that's on you. I got it straight from the kid's mouth, and I'm running with it."

"Max. I don't have any idea what you're saying, just get over here as fast as you can, Bull will be here soon."

"Uh-uh, I'm stashing the kid some place safe."

"Max, I'm warning you . . ." but the phone was dead.

Chapter 10

Bull blew through Duck Key heading south twenty miles an hour over the limit. He was deep in thought, running all the angles, trying to work through what was going on. Who would want to kill Sheila? Why was Jack moved up to the Everglades Correctional Unit? Hell, that was state, not county. It wasn't until he crossed Vaca Cut into Marathon when he picked up the rain that he backed off the gas. Marathon was notorious for working speed traps. Once up on the Seven Mile Bridge he jammed the pedal down. Daylight was burning.

Forty-five minutes later he pulled in behind the Sand Bar. The year before, Jack had gone off on a binge and stayed drunk for three months. He tried to drink himself to death and in the process damn near lost everything he had. He signed over the *Island Queen* to Bull, made Coco half owner of the Sand Bar, and bought Lamont and Cookie a small two-bedroom cinderblock house over off Roosevelt. The coup-de-grace though was giving up his apartment over the bar and moving into a small conch house down the alley that ran between Banana and Duval. Coco moved into the apartment over the bar, so she could keep a close eye on the business below, and Jack went out and got drunk, and stayed out until Mama Obi got her hands on him and hung a gris-gris around his neck. Bull didn't believe in all that Voodoo mumbo jumbo but damned if the boy didn't sober up and get on with the business of living.

Coco was waiting for him at the back-screen door that led into the bar's kitchen. The smell of frying food made him hungry. Cookie stood over the grill, a dozen patties were sizzling on the gas grill, fries bubbled and popped in the submerged grease basket, and a huge pot of gumbo simmered on a back burner, along with another pot of conch chowder.

"Mister C, throw me a grouper basket together with a mess of fries, would you please? I haven't had a bite since oh-dark-thirty."

To say Cookie was black didn't do him justice, he was blacker than black, polished ebony with a reddish sheen to him at times, and blue at others. At the moment, he was focused on the meat on the grill and just nodded his head. "Cup a gumbo on the side," Cookie added, as an afterthought.

"You were reading my mind, Mister C. Make it so," Bull answered.

"Thank God, you're here, things are getting more and more upsetting by the hour," Coco said, motioning Bull through the swinging doors into the bar.

"You're on target, Coco, it's starting to spin out of control. You wouldn't believe where Sheriff Polk has sent Jack," he didn't wait for an answer, "The bastard had a deputy run him up to ECI. That place is the end of the road for every bad con in the state of Florida. Jack hasn't even been tried yet. Judge Powers stopped any bail just on the sheriff's plea, and now, Jack's in the crapper."

"Oh, Bull, I'm just sick about everything that's happening. It doesn't make sense. I don't know which way to turn."

"First thing is that we need to get Jinx over here and do what he has to do to get Jack out of state custody. He didn't kill Sheila, it's just payback from Polk."

"What should we do about Renée, she didn't show up for work today. Scarlet picks her up every morning for work. Today, she called Renée to tell her she was on her way, but she didn't answer. She drove over to check, thinking she may have overslept, but she didn't answer the door. With all the crazy stuff going on she was worried and peeked through her bedroom blinds and her bed hadn't been slept in."

"If you haven't called the cops yet, don't. We don't know what Polk's game is and until I know more about why Jack is being held in ECI, I don't want to do anything that will hurt him."

Coco ran worried fingers through her hair and turned her head to hide her concern. She was a strong woman that had seen every mean thing life could throw at a woman, but this was becoming too much.

"I'm going to call Bill, he can help us."

Captain Bill Price was Senior Agent for Florida's Bureau of Investigation and Coco's boyfriend or companion. Nobody knew which, including Coco.

"May not be a bad idea. Something dangerous is happening and I think Jack is caught in the middle of it."

Coco answered her cell phone on the second ring looking at the caller ID, "Lamont, talk to me?"

"He ain't here, Miss Coco."

"What do you mean? Are you talking about Blue?"

"Yes, Ma'am. They say he went missing at the midnight bed check, him and his belongings. The lady said she called his parole officer and reported him missing. They're going to pull his parole and when they find him he's going back to Raiford, for sure."

"Swing over and pick up Jinx, then get back here as quick as you can, things are getting crazier."

She hung up and looked at Bull, "This is crazy, but Blue may be the one that killed Sheila."

"What? No way, he's too much of a lightweight, just look at him, he couldn't hurt a Key's chicken. Just look at those baby blues, they look more like a pretty girl's than a man's."

"Well, you may be wrong on this one. Max found Mikey and he told Max that the man that killed his mother had blue eyes."

"Max found Mikey! Why didn't you tell me first off? Jeez, I've been worried sick over that kid."

"Well, he found him, but now he's playing games with me. He says he's not bringing Mikey here to the Sand Bar because Blue might try something to hurt Mikey."

"That's crazy. This is the safest place for the kid right now. Where did he take him?"

"Someplace safe is all he said. Knowing Max that could be anywhere from Bahia Honda camp grounds to McDonald's."

Cookie brought Bull's food and set it on the bar mumbling about how white folks was holding him down and how they expect the poor colored folks to be waiting on them hand and foot.

"Can't even come get your own food," he said, and clucked loudly. "Martin Luther be right about all them civilian rights and such."

"I'm sorry, Mister C. I got tied up talking to Coco and forgot all about my food. We were talking about Sheila and Blue . . ."

"Blue? I done forgot, Miss Coco. That Blue boy come by last night when I was closing up the kitchen, and scrubbing things down. He liked to scare the squirts out of me the way he came sneaking in the back door. There I was listening to my church music and the next thing, he's standing over my shoulder all crazy-eyed. Look like he was high on that ganga weed them Jamaica boys smoke."

"What did he want, Cookie? What time was this?" she questioned.

"It was way after all y'all gone home after being over to the court to bring Mister Jack home, must have been close to two-thirty is my best guess."

"What did he say, Mister C?" Bull asked.

"He made me give him some paper and pencil to write it down, he said it was important and that it just might save his life. He went off to blubbering and crying the blues about nobody ever believed him in his life, not even his own grandma what raised him. I told him I knowed 'xactly what he was talking about, my own momma turned me in for a award . . ."

"You mean a reward, don't you," Bull said, caught up in the story.

"Yes, sir, that is 'xactly what she did . . ."

"Cookie, what did he say?" Coco pushed, trying to refocus the conversation to get it back on track.

"I got it right here on the back of that order for three cheeseburger baskets come in late before closing and then they changed their mind . . ."

"Jesus wept," Coco groaned, "Give it to me," she snatched it out of his hand and began reading it aloud,

'Mister Jack. I'm running. I just can't take the fall for something I didn't do. I know everybody is going to think I killed Sheila, but I didn't. I loved her, even though she didn't love me. She loved somebody else that she kept a secret, but I know who it is. I seen him pick her up on the corner from work and at the corner of her apartment a few times. He's the one that killed her, not me. If they catch me, I'll be in prison again. I would rather be dead than back in that place. It's more dangerous in there than it is out on the street so I'm running, and I won't be back. Mathew Turner, Blue', it was signed.

She let her hand drop and dabbed at an eye, "I am so tired of all the hurt and anguish in this town. Every person down here is at the end of the line, no more places to run or hide. It just never stops."

Cookie stopped her from her sorrow, "You can't think that way, Miss Coco. For some of us it's a new beginning. Why, if I didn't have you and Mister Jack, I'd still be in prison. Praise God for folks like y'all. Me, I count myself as lucky every day. I got a house, a job, friends, people that love me. What did I have before I come down here? I'll tell you straight up, and I won't lie to you, I didn't have nothing and no prospects in life neither. I stabbed a man and killed him dead, and I'm sorry every day of my life he died. I ain't sorry I gutted him, because he earned it, but I am sorry he died and caused me so much pain in my life."

"You're right, we don't have time to be feeling sorry for ourselves, we have people in trouble," Coco dabbed at her eyes and tossed her head, '*Don't worry, Jack, I'll work it out,*' she thought, biting down hard on her lip, casting off the moment.

Chapter 11

Clouds scurried overhead scattering rain as they went, the air in the taxi was close and smelled of sweat, old food, and ground in grime.

"It stinks in here, Mithster," Mikey said, crinkling his nose. "Did you make a wythe kwispie butt in here?" He said in a child's lisp.

"What?" Max glanced at Mikey through the rearview mirror.

Max had been in a deep moment of smugness. He had solved the murder mystery and didn't even break a sweat.

"Wythe kwispie butt, you know, when you accidently make noise come out of your bottom. Momma always said that you should always say excuse me when they come out by accident, especially if they thmell. Momma's were always thmelly, and she never said excuse me. She said mine were 'sgusting, but I know mine aren't as bad as hers, I like mine. Want to see? I can make it happen anytime I want, 'thpecially around girls at school, they start running and screaming, but I know they like it."

"Stop with the dirty talk, and no, I don't want to smell your farts."

Max was trying to digest what he had just been told by a six-year-old about his mother's bodily functions. People today were teaching their kids too much too early. If he ever said something like that to his mom she would have smacked him into next week. When he was a kid if you had gas, you saved it until you were in the toilet, or in a big crowd so no one would know who did it.

He almost blew by the Shark Key turnoff and whipped across the lane in front of an oncoming eighteen-wheeler. *'What the hell?'* Two Sheriff's cars parked across from the entrance into the Key. The trucker laid on his airhorn blasting a trail of earsplitting noise as he whizzed by barely missing Max. Max flipped him off and smiled.

"Love to piss off those big guys, they think they own the road."

"You said an ugly, Mithster,"

"You bet I did, kid. You hang with me, I'll teach you words like you never heard before. Some of 'em will get you places in this world."

He checked if the deputies were going to bust him for pulling in front of the truck like that. *'Nah, just doing what cops do, fucking off on the clock.'*

Max stopped at the gate and watched the same rent-a-cop step out of the gatehouse into the rain.

"Semper Fi, Marine," the muscled guard recognized Max.

"Rikers, Marine" Max answered back thinking, *'What's with the semper fi, some kind of Pig Latin Marine mumbo gumbo?'* he asked himself.

"You here to pick up Mister Rocket? I don't have any pickup notice here on the list, but that don't mean a thing, seems he's got so many people coming and going I guess he forgets to tell security."

The guard leaned into the window and spotted Mikey in the back seat and grunted.

"I know it ain't none of my business but who's the boy?"

"Him, he's my nephew. I'm teaching him the business. I'm thinking I'll be coming into some money pretty soon and will need good people working for me."

"That sounds nice, family has to stick together. I was just worried that maybe one of Mister Rocket's people sent for the kid," the guard said, giving Max a wink.

"What ya mean, sent for a kid? You talking what I think you're talking?"

"I ain't talking nothing, I'm just saying lots of crazy people coming and going night and day anytime at Mister Rocket's home. When he's off on one of his music tours it's as quiet as a church mouse around his place, except for the help." He was obviously nervous talking about Billy Rocket. "I got a lady friend that works for him, she says when he leaves it takes her and a couple of other gals forever to clean that place, she says she has to hose down some of those rooms from all the mess him and his friends leave behind."

"Yeah? Sounds like my kind of party," Max sniggered. "Back in the day, I hung out on 42nd Street in Manhattan and seen every corruption a man could see in a lifetime. Talk about your dames and atrocities, *Ba-Boom!*"

"Well, I've never been to New York, but I've been to Yokohama and seen a thing or two, and I had my share of it. Sometimes I wish I had stayed in the Corp, just so I could pull liberty in Yokohama or Bangkok again. Woo-wee, those were righteous times."

"Look, I'd like to sit here and shoot the breeze with you, but I have business to tend to with Mister Rocket. Don't call him ahead of me pulling in out there, I want to surprise him."

"No problem, I won't say a word, besides, I don't know your name anyway."

"Simms, Max Simms. 007. This cab is my office, it fools the bad guys and unsuspecting into thinking I'm just a shmuck cabbie. Don't you believe it. I like you, pal, maybe there'll be a place in my organization once I close this case I'm working on. What's your name?"

"Ray Bodine, and I'll take you up on that offer too, this is a dead-end job. I'm just marking time here until a career opportunity comes along."

"I'll put your name on the list, Ray. The top positions are going to go fast, but I'll put you in for one."

"Thank you, Mister Simms, I appreciate that. Just holler out if you need any references or historical information on me . . . and watch it out there, Mister Rocket has had a party going since last night and it don't look like it's stopping any time soon."

"Thanks, Ray, I might be in there for a while. I'm overdue for some serious partying."

Max took his time driving past the imposing homes on either side of the paved street, each compound sitting on at least an acre of coral backing onto canals leading out to the Gulf. Peeks of wealth could be seen through huge ornate wrought iron gates with paver driveways lined with tropical flora and sporty cars. Enormous yachts were visible pulling on jumper lines ready for a sunset cruise.

As he approached the end of the road, he became apprehensive about something, but he couldn't put his finger on it. He was a product of Brooklyn streets where you learned to listed to your inner voice and act accordingly.

That voice was beating out drums of warning, but why? He pulled to the side of the road and held the brake down. He sat staring at the imposing home where one of the most well-known people in the world lived . . . well, maybe at one time he was well-known.

Max sat there thinking to himself . . . *'But still, Billy Rocket was hot snot among old-time diehard heavy metal fans. The man was still a millionaire, wasn't he? How could he still be living in the life if he wasn't loaded, right? All those rock stars had groupies that partied all the time, didn't they? What was the big deal? The big deal, Max, is that you are here to swipe the briefcase of money from this guy, not get Mikey to a safe place. Mikey was just an excuse to get inside, the kid had his whole life ahead of him to make it big. This was his time to score, there was enough money in that briefcase to set him up in a nice place back in the old neighborhood and be somebody. Men would walk by and tip their hat, women would flirt with him, young punks would ask for advice on life, and boy, did he have a bucket load of advice to give out. He would be somebody, he just needed to jump start it.*

He knew too, that no matter how many years go by, once you're a con you're always a con. Life had played him a lucky hand once. Why couldn't it do it again? The last hand dealt almost cost him a life bounce inside Sing-Sing Correctional Facility, north of New York City on the bank of the Hudson River where it was so cold in the winter that inmates lost fingers to frostbite from hanging on their cell bars. He was waiting his sentencing and facing a life sentence for murder in the commission of a robbery. If he hadn't gotten lost in the paperwork in Rikers while waiting for a trial date, he would be in the Big Slam right now. But instead, some office weenie screwed up on his papers and he got lost in the system . . . for three years he stayed lost working in the city's prison kitchens. Then one day, they called his name over the PA system to report to the admin office where they apologized about having lost his paperwork and they really weren't sure why he was there. They had him sign a paper promising not to sue the city of New York and to just go away and be a good boy. They even fronted him with a new suit and three hundred bucks. I call that luck. Anybody would. No, he was thinking of how he could get his mitts on the briefcase with the cash in it. Yeah, it was worth the risk.'

He hit the gas and entered thru the open gate where a lazy fat guy waved him through. Max made brief eye contact with the guy and knew he was stoned out of his gourd. He pulled up on the lawn next to a shiny black Humvee adorned with everything polished chrome gadgets one could imagine, jacked up so high the passengers could sprain an ankle getting in and out. Sleek luxury cars were double parked along the drive, overflow parking covered the grounds like a rich man's junk yard. The fact that his pink family-van stuck out like a naked fat boy at a Richard Simon's get-together didn't bother Max at all. He straightened his bow tie in the mirror and turned to Mikey.

"Hey, kid, I'm going inside to make arrangements with a very important man to keep you safe, so nobody can hurt you. You stay right here and don't go nowhere. You do like I say, I'll smell your Rice Krispies. Okay?"

"Wow! You promise?"

"Didn't I say I would? Sheesh." Max said, as he got out and locked the door behind him.

Without hesitating, Max bounced up the portico steps and through the large heavy iron and beveled glass double doors. The smell of weed, laughter and music hit him like a hammer blow before he even had his bearings. A woman, more like a girl, ran by with bare breasts bouncing, giggling as a punk with half his head shaved, the other half a neon purple chased after her. Somewhere deeper in the house, he could hear Billy and the band pounding out one of his oldies. He rubbed at his burning eyes and took shallow breath's as he mingled his way across the cavernous room. In the huge chef's kitchen, a couple were fornicating on the granite island counter top as others looked on, some simply oblivious to them, raided the fridge or munched from bags of chips. Max was watching engrossed at the couple doing the dirty as someone grabbed him from behind and ran their hands into his front pockets. Two things happened, he screamed like a woman and second, he grabbed to make sure his wallet chain was still hooked to his pant loop, satisfied that he wasn't being rolled, he swung around into the arms of a six-foot-tall gorgeous redhead.

"Did I scare you, Daddy," the knockout slurred through dreamy eyes.

Max was stuck for an answer, as he watched the woman stick her tongue out first one side then the other wagging and twining the two halves like wet snakes.

"The fuck!" He stammered in disbelief. The broad had a split tongue. "What ya go and do that for?"

The redhead ignored him, bent and kissed his mouth, "I think I found my forever man, the man of my dreams," she said, then bent down and licked his face from chin to nose.

It was the most bizarre thing that he had ever experienced, having a chick lick his nose on both sides at the same time. He pulled away, she was about to get too personal and run one or both halves up his nostrils. Max felt used, he couldn't believe this was happening to him. The dame was abusing him . . . and that nose ring was just plain scary.

"Uh, Miss, you need to stop what you're doing, you really need to stop. I practice Tai Chi and I'm not afraid to use it."

"God, you animal," she moaned. "You make me crazy talking like that. Tai Chi me, right here, right now . . ." she pulled her tube top down to her waist and swung her 40-D breasts back and forth seductively which happened to be at his eye level.

Max's head swung like a metronome in time to the beautiful breasts. He was quickly rethinking making a quick exit out the back door and make his getaway. This could turn into a meaningful relationship, maybe not so much the tongue, but the boobs were keepers.

"You have a name, honey?" He asked lustily. Just the asking of her name gave him courage.

"Name, no, I don't have a name. Names are so . . . so . . . extra."

"Wow! That is so transnormal," Max said, as he breathed deeply of the trail of smoke rising from the blunt between her fingers. He couldn't remember ever feeling this good. He stuck his nose closer to the burning weed and breathed deep. It was a moment of beauty as he took the redhead in his arms and began to dance to some forgotten tune from an old black and white movie he had seen as a kid.

"Let's grab a couple of beers and find a quiet place to become friends," he said, as she held the joint down to his mouth and he pulled in a huge lung full of the bitter tasting smoke.

Abruptly, she pulled away from him but left her top down, breasts exposed.

"Come on, I know the perfect place. Forget the beer, I'll get us something much better," she said and almost pulled him off his feet, as she made a bee line for the dining room.

In the center on an enormous dining table sat a large dinner plate on a golden charger. On the plate was a mound of white powder that had small butter knives stuck in and around it. Max knew the powder had to be cocaine and for just a moment he fought the urge to run, but not being a strong man, plus the promise of the redhead, he helped her scoop several ounces onto a saucer. Red, as he thought of his new love, balanced the saucer with one hand and cupped one of his butt cheeks with the other.

"Come with me, my little rodent," Red slurred.

"Yes, my heart. Lead the way."

Red led the way down a seemingly endless maze of corridors and hallways talking in some foreign tongue as they went. Suddenly it occurred to him she was singing Bon Jovi's *'Livin' on a Prayer'*, one of his all-time favorites.

"Damn Red, you doing Bon Jovi and the whole group all at the same time. I'm stunned. I'll tell you straight up, I wasn't overwhelmed with the tongue action at first but now, I'm thinking we can make some money.

Damn straight, if this is big as I think, I might even get mine cut too and we can do a double billing, maybe front for Billy" He laughed at the image that sprang to mind with Red and he with split tongue's trying to sing a Twisted Sister jam.

Red stopped in front of a door and held a finger up to her lips, and went, "Thhhh, be twyit."

He whispered back, and said, "Otay." He clasped a hand over his mouth to muffle giggle.

She pushed the door open into a dark bedroom, ambient light coming from the storm blowing outside peeked around the edges of the wide veined closed plantation shutters casting dreamy shadows around the room. The musk smell of expensive men's cologne made Max sneeze. Red closed the door behind them and pulled Max into her arms and kissed him on the lips forcing his mouth open. She began to moan and sway.

He was in heaven, never in his life would he ever imaging being kissed by two tongues at the same time. It made his little cabdriver perk up. His fingers fumbled with his clip-on bowtie and the top button. A flash crossed his mind that he needed to pick up his cleaning later in the day, this was his last clean shirt.

Red pulled back and looked into his eyes, and whispered, "My little rodent, I need you now. Take me . . . take me, now."

"Sheesh, slow down, honey, I got buttons here for Christ sakes." He finally gave up and tore at his shirt, popping all the buttons after the third try. His arms fell to his sides letting the shirt flutter to the floor. He went after his belt with a vengeance as he watched Red slip off her shorts, 'The Fuck! She ain't wearing any skivvies.'

He kicked his boxer shorts off as she pulled him to the edge of the bed, she grabbed him by his quivering shoulders and fell back bringing him with her. She wrapped her long legs around him and guided him magically with her hips, moaning and singing gibberish, her eyes were a lusty glaze. He was on fire, this was going to be the finest few minutes of his life. His mind was on overload. Adrenalin raged through his body, testosterone had the little cabdriver in first gear . . . almost in overdrive . . . it was going to happen . . .

"Renée! What the fuck! What are you doing here?" Max exclaimed, when he discovered they weren't alone.

Renée Carter was on the far side of the king size bed, asleep or unconscious, he couldn't tell which. He peered sharply in the gloom and scoped out her nude body. He thought maybe she had been beat up, for sure one eye was swollen closed, snot was bubbling out of her nose and she snored quietly.

He pulled away from Red and crawled across the big bed to Renée. His little cabdriver forgotten, this was serious shit. A syringe hung from her right arm, seemingly forgotten, the plunger was bottomed out. He put his hand on her bare chest to feel a heartbeat and quickly pulled it away, *'that was disgusting,'* he thought, the girl's OD'd and he's copping a feel. He lifted an eyelid into huge pupils that reminded him of a cat he hated once.

"I got to get you out of here, sweetheart or you ain't going to make it."

"Rodent . . . come to momma," Red moaned.

"Shut up, can't you see we got a emergency here. Put some frigging clothes on before someone comes in and thinks we're doing something. It ain't decent, you, me, and Renée all three *in flagrante delicto* or whatever that word is Jinx uses when he's all wound up and starts talking that lawyer mumbo gumbo."

"Come here, baby, momma needs it."

"Here, ya crazy dame, snort some more of this stuff, it'll give you whatever your craving."

He bounced himself off the bed and scurried around gathering his togs, *'fucking shirt's ruined.'* He pulled his boxer's up high on his small hips and cast around for his trousers, found them and checked first thing that his wallet was still in the pocket and the chain attached to the belt loop. He knew you could never trust a dame no matter how beautiful she was, and this one was a knock out. If he had his cell phone he would snap a couple quick photos of her, but he had left it in the car. He caught an image of himself in the closet door mirrors and winked, he was on a roll. He saved Mikey from a life on the run and now he's rescuing Renée from drugs. Jackie and the boys were going to eat their hearts out when they see what he'd done without their help. *'F'em, if you got it, flaunt it'*

He slid one of the mirrored doors open and gasped into the huge walk-in closet, double rows of Billy's shirts and show costumes hung from ceiling to floor, all hung in color coordinated graduated colors. *'And the shoes! Dude!'* He looked over his shoulder and slid the door closed with him still inside. He lovingly fingered the different materials and chose a subdued blackish blue silk shirt with blue sequins sewn all over the lapel. He slipped it on and got a boner. The matching pants had the cabdriver erect and ready. He gave the trouser legs more than a couple of folds up to fit his short frame, and went to his knees for matching shoes. He narrowed the hunt down to a pair of platform ankle boots that were much too big for his tiny feet.

A line of light caught his attention in the back of the closet that shouldn't be there. He stuck his head closer to the back wall and saw it was a narrow door. He listened for any sound but didn't detect any. He pushed gently, and the door swung open effortlessly. The bright fluorescent lights made him squint. Once they were adjusted he pulled back into the closet then slowly peeked out. He was looking at a counting room just like the one he had seen on that tour behind the scenes at the

Taj Mahal Hotel Casino in Atlantic City when he and his bowling team took a bus trip down for a few days of slots and buffets.

The room smelled of Cup-O-Noodles and weed. He sneezed loudly and wiped his nose with the back of his hand then onto the sequined shirt, not taking his eyes off the money stacked on the table in the center of the room. He looked over his shoulder to make sure nobody was sneaking up on him and, staying on all fours, made it to the table. Two tables on either side of a caged metal door was stacked with kilo blocks of cocaine. A third table must be the bagging table, he thought. Plastic bins were filled with small inch square sleeves of the white powder and large cakes of blow.

His heart was going to explode from fear and excitement, he didn't know what to do first. He went into action. The first thing was to throw the bolts on the three locks on the steel door, the next was to empty one of the plastic tubs onto the table careful not to let any of the smack fall to the floor, the next was to start packing stacks of money into the tub. His hands were shaking like a kid's first time squeezing a pair of tits. His days of burglaring came back to him and he calmed down, becoming aware of his surroundings and what he was doing. He stopped packing the money when he saw the stacks were mixed bills, he spotted the hundreds at the end of the table and went for them. Once filled, he shoved the tub through the back door into the closet, checked to make sure the sliding doors were still closed and shoved the bucket farther away from the secret entrance.

Back inside the counting room, he tore open a bag of coke and began pouring a trail from the table across the floor to the steel door, then around the door itself. Back at the coke table he shook out the last of the powder, licked his finger tip, and wrote in the powder,

'You been holding out on me, Billy Boy. You've been a bad boy and you know what happens to bad boys.' Sheriff Polk

Max stood back to admire his genius, wiped his finger tip on his front of Billy's shirt and unbolted the steel door locks, scurried across the room and pulled the secret door closed behind him, grinning all the way. Back in the bedroom, Red was gone along with the saucer of coke. He tiptoed across the room and peeked out into the hallway. A couple were arguing about something further down the hallway. He closed the door and surveyed the room. How was he going to get Renée out to the taxi? Thunder rumbled outside reminding him of what a crappy day it was. That was his answer, they would go out the window and around the house. He would put her in the van with Mikey and come back for the tub of money, *Ba Boom!*

"Come on, sugar, we're going for a walk." Max pulled Renée up into a sitting position, bent and hoisted her over his small shoulder. He wobbled under the deadweight and fell backwards.

"This ain't going to work, sweetheart."

He pulled the comforter from the bed and rolled Renée onto it then dragged her to the window. Lightning flashed followed by an atomic boom of thunder a moment later, the rain fell in sheets. Max fiddled with the window for a moment, put his back into it and it slid open, then he fought with the screen, finally giving up, he cut the screen with his pocket knife. Using all his strength, he got Renée up on the sill then shoved her the rest of the way out. She landed in a heap among a bed of ferns. Max was out the window right behind her dragging the quilt with him. He closed the window tight, took a moment to catch his breath thinking for the umpteenth time that he needed to join a boxing club to get his wind back. When he fought Golden Gloves as a boy he could go six, maybe seven rounds and not break a sweat, even though he was smoking a pack of Lucky's a day.

He laid out the cover and rolled sleeping beauty on it and began to pull. The blanket cushioned her ride over the crushed coral but had Max slipping and sliding wearing Billy's oversized ankle boots.

"Hell with this," he said, as he pulled of the shoes and tossed them on the naked body.

That worked better, he could dig his toes into the coral and began to make good time, even though the sharp gravel cut his feet with each step. The thought of the tub of money motivated him to not think about the pain shooting up from his bloody feet.

One of the portico guards wasn't sure what he was seeing until Max got closer then, he began to laugh.

"You playing Santa, man?" The punk grinned.

"Fuck you," Max said, out of breath. "Give me a hand, don't just stand there looking at the broad. Ain't you never seen a naked woman before?"

"Sure, lots of them, but never one that's being pulled across a yard on a blanket by Little Boy Blue. The outfit doesn't work, dude. You need to go easy on that shit they're serving up inside, it ruins a man's ability to judge basic colors. I can see you hit that shit hard. I ain't judging, I'm just sayin', dude."

"Stop with the jabbering and give me a hand, Billy wants this chick off the grounds post adios, you with me?"

They made fast work of dragging the blanket to the van. Max actually had backed off and left the heavy pulling to goofball that had an Uzi in one hand and a handful of blanky in the other.

"That's far enough, Rambo. I got it from here," he said, pulling out a wad of hundreds he had stuck in his pocket back in the closet.

"Here, buy yourself a course in keeping your yap shut." He peeled off three one hundred-dollar bills and tucked them in the man's shirt pocket. "Monkey no see, Monkey no talk, capiche?"

"Wow, man, that's generous of you. Monkey no remember anything either for a couple more of those sweet honeybees."

"You're killing me, Rambo. I'll go another two, but if I hear anything back, there's going to be some serious consequences and repercussions."

"I ain't never seen anybody dressed like Little Boy Blue pulling a naked lady on a blanket across the yard. Trust me, nobody would believe me anyway."

Max wrestled with Renée across the last few feet of rough coral. Holding her sagging body he slid back the vans side door and flopped her inside. Mikey, give me hand, grab her hands and I'll take her feet," he struggled getting her butt off the running board and onto the van's floor. "Mikey, grab her hands and pull, boy."

A cold chill tickled Max's neck, "Mikey? Mikey, where are you?"

Mikey was gone.

Chapter 12

The wire cage was constructed of heavy gauge cyclone fencing, the kind they used to pen fighting dogs that couldn't be bitten through no matter how much the animal was taunted and teased. The cages at ECI Camp 7 each swung suspended a foot off the ground like a bird cage, prisoners passing by were expected to give the cage a spin or be punished themselves if they didn't.

Jack was balled tight in the smallest of the cages. His knees were pulled up to his chin and arms wrapped around them tight. He ached all over, a stabbing pain shot through his chest with every breath, possibly from a broken rib. Flying insects covered the bloody wounds around his damaged nose and mouth. It throbbed where his tooth had been knocked out. With each breath, the air sent a bolt of pain through his brain.

He had been in tight fixes before, but this was beyond a fix, this was torture. He wasn't sure if he would survive this trip. Another round with Mister Toby and he would be dead. There was no way he could be beaten like that again. One thing for sure was that if he got the chance, Toby would be the first to go down, with Boss Dalton being the second.

Jack closed his mind, letting his thoughts trail off into darkness, somewhere between awareness and precious healing. Snatches of the last 24 hours ran through his mind like flashcards demanding answers that were printed just out of sight on the other side. He gave up after what seemed like an eternity and slipped into blissful sleep.

He came awake with the cage spinning and swinging. Boss Dalton stood off watching as a bare-chested man wound the cage up and then let it go to spin wildly. A dozen other men in rag pants laughed along with Dalton. Jack threw up bloody bile as the torturous spinning continued.

"Enough!" Boss Dalton bellowed with a chopping motion of his ham sized fist. The ragtag crowd stopped immediately on the command. Jack was seeing triple of everything as the cage door was opened and he was dragged out.

"Walk me a line, boy," Dalton demanded. "You walk me a line and you can sleep with these beauties here. If you can't walk a line, you're going back in the cage until you can. Right boys?" he said, over his shoulder.

A desperate chorus of "Yes, sir Boss man . . . Amen, Boss . . . Praise God, Boss . . . I say he needs to go back in, Boss Dalton . . ."

Dalton slashed his hand down again and the crowd went silent.

"Toby, draw a line."

The huge trustee snapped too and began drawing a line with his big toe. The line ran for about fifteen feet when Dalton yelled for him to stop.

"Get your ass up and toe that line. I ain't saying pull nothing, you got to run your toe down that rut Toby made, now get to it before I slap your lilly white ass back in that rock-a-bye cradle."

Jack heard everything Dalton had said and wanted to comply but couldn't pull it all together. His head spun one way and his legs another, he went down in a heap.

The crowd was cheering and calling out bets, some rooted for him, others against.

"I'll give you one more try, Marsh, then back into the swing."

Jack wobbled to his feet and carefully stared down at the small trench. He put his left big toe in it and began tracing Toby's line. He forced his head to clear but still mangled the effort. He took several deep breaths while shaking his head. His stomach heaved, and bile dribbled down the corners of his mouth, he shook his head again, and began taking baby steps. He made it to the end of the dirt line and everyone cheered, except Boss Dalton.

"You were faking it, Marsh, weren't you? You were just playing at being dizzy."

Jack kept his face blank, as he stood staring at the big man.

"Why . . . you punk, don't you look at me like that. I'll drop you hard. Get on your knees," he commanded.

Jack gladly fell to his knees, he didn't see the kick coming, but when it landed on his kidney he screamed in pain and fell in a ball of agony.

"You cheated, Marsh. You ain't going to get away with cheating me like that. I'm the boss here and I just decided you ain't never leaving me. I'm going to work you like a dog, I'm going to be watching you every minute of every day. You think you hurt now, you ain't felt pain like I got in store for you." Boss Dalton growled.

Some of the older hands cringed at his wrath, they had survived this man's insane tortures themselves and didn't want to be anywhere near someone that was going to be put to the test, a test that many failed.

"String him up, Toby. I want him to hang every night until I say otherwise. Tell the cook, nothing for this boy except piss and puke for a week. He'll be going out with the girl squad at sunrise, you tell Mister Goodbar when he comes in, I want him to lean on this boy, lean hard."

"What about togs, Boss. You want me to get him something out of the barrel to wear. We ain't got no hats but I can find something for him to cover up that puny little worm with."

"He ain't earned togs yet, Mister Toby. Let him get a little burn on him for a few days to darken him up. Warden Cotton come out here and see a lilly white ass like that walking around he's libel to think I've been slacking off. Nope, let him sizzle a bit."

"Yes, suh, Boss."

"And, Toby, hose down that redbone nigga y'all brought in today and send him up to the house. Make sure he's clean, I don't want to be smelling nothing but that ivory soap."

"Yes, suh, Boss, hose the redbone down good and soap him up, yes suh."

Jack's dirt crusted fingertips barely brushed the ground as he hung upside down. His head felt like exploding as it throbbed with each beat of his heart. The full weight of his body bore down on him making it even more difficult to breathe. He forced himself to breath shallow to keep the pain at bay, but even this didn't eliminate all the agony. He was sure that he wasn't going to get out alive, there just wasn't anything like this that would even be believed. If the outside world knew about this place, they wouldn't believe it. It made GITMO a daycare center. This was straight out of some Hollywood thriller, or something out of Dostoevsky.

The day turned into evening, Jack watched as lines of half-naked men trudged tiredly in from different directions and collapsed around the camp. It was eerie, clouds of flies circled around the prisoner's heads like satanic halos, some shooed at the pests, but most just ignored them too tired to care. Jack used his fingertips to steady himself, he couldn't believe the specter like figures filing past him. None of them even gave him a glance. Most of the skeletal figures were covered in runny sores, pruned flesh from being submerged all day in the brackish water gave their calves and feet a green caste, none of the men wore shoes.

He watched as the men slumped to the ground with grunts and groan in complete exhaustion

"Up! On your feet. Get up!" Several trustees bellowed, swatting the inmates as they pushed through the men.

Slowly the men began to form into three groups across the grounds facing the raised hut. Mister Toby and two other trustees yelled and prodded the men into platoon formations. Once the trustees appeared satisfied, they took up a position in front of their platoon. The men swayed in the ranks, occasionally, one would start to fall then catch himself and pull back upright

Boss Dalton strode out of the hut onto the porch in a fresh uniform looking more like Field Marshall Idi Amin DaDa than a psychotic redneck sociopath.

"Report," he called out, in a parade field command.

"Alpha Squad all present except for Leonard Jackson. Sir."

"Bravo Squad, all here and ready to go on watch." Groans rose from the ranks.

"Charlie Squad mostly hear, got some laggards coming in."

"Mister Leon, talk to me later about your missing inmate. I'll need to report him missing if he doesn't show up by morning. I suspect a gator got him."

"No sir, it was a moccasin that got him. We were working that patch of mangrove over by the inlet. I specs' he be gone by now. Y'all told us don't bring 'em back if it goin' to be a burden on ta' others."

"You did good, Mister Leon. If a man can't carry his own weight I won't cut him slack. That's just the way we roll in this camp. Maybe some of the other camps might go soft, but I'm not. There's not a mutt among you that doesn't belong here, your ass is mine. You suck it up, you live. You go soft or get yourself in a bind, that's on you. I'll feed you and clothe you but I ain't going to coddle you. Besides there's lots of boys needing sent here. Major Cotton's urging me to bear down a little more on you sorry assed convicts, he says I'm not turning the inventory fast enough. He says I'm getting soft, well I ain't. Just to prove it, I want all squads up on watch tonight, one-hundred percent up. I catch anyone sleeping, they'll go in the cage."

"Na, Boss, I can't do it . . . I can't do this . . . I'd rather be dead . . ."

"Who said that? Who was that. Was that in your squad, Goodbar?"

"Yes, suh, it was Moore, suh."

"Mister Toby, string Moore up, and string Goodbar up alongside him. I demand discipline from my trustees. You're out Goodbar, give your yellow armband to Little Billy, you're out. I been watching Billy, he'll dust those boys up."

"Don't do it, Boss, you know what'll happen to me if I go back on the line. I drove those boys hard, Boss. They'll kill me first chance they get. I'll straighten up, Boss, don't put me on the line, Please, Boss, I'm begging."

"Shut up, Goodbar, if you can't hold your own against a bunch of sissies then you deserve to go down."

Mister Toby called out for help with marching Moore and Goodbar over to where Jack swung watching the insanity playout. Within moments the two men swung suspended from metal poles within arm's length of Jack. Moore was crying, clearly terrified. Goodbar rocked back and forth on his tether with his arms wrapped protectively around his chest.

"Welcome to Oz," Jack offered, and quickly grimaced in pain. He spat a glob of bloody snot and tried to remain still.

The night fell over the camp quickly, one moment it was a dusky fusion of shadow and then blackness. The only light came from Boss Dalton's hut, the dark swallowed the ambient light from the windows giving the impression that the hut floated on a sea of black nothingness. The mosquitos came first. Out of the night they arrived like fighter jets over an enemy island. They buzzed, strafed and bit nonstop. Jack fought back but finally gave up. The tender parts of his body were ground zero for every insect of the night, flies attached themselves to bloody and bruised abrasions. Persistent no-see-ems bit at his exposed back and armpits. Something stung his balls and he convulsed.

"*AHHHGGG!*" he screamed out in a moment of complete insanity and grabbed himself. "I've got to get out of here," he said, into the blackness.

"You ain't going nowhere white boy, the onliest place you goin' is to the swamp."

Chapter 13

Max sat in the backseat of the cab with Renée's head in his lap, patting her as he thought out what to do. Mikey was gone, the little fuck.

'I told him to stay inside the taxi no matter what. Does that mean someone spotted him and snatched him? Maybe the kid had to take a whiz and stepped off into the bushes and got lost, couldn't find his way back, that don't sound right, this kid was a smooth operator. Hell, he lived out of a dumpster for a couple of day. I know winos in Manhattan that ain't that smart, unless it's winter time and then you gotta fight for a space inside one of those cans.'

He looked down at Renée, lifted an eyelid, and let it drop.

'What if she dies. Yeah, and what about my box of money in the closet. What would Jackie do, go after the kid, save the dame, or get the money?' he thought for a moment, *'fuck it, I'm going for the money.'*

He knew if he went back the way he came that dopy guard would think something was fishy. He cut to the right, ignoring the rain soaking his taxi cap, knowing the cardboard bill would be all out of shape, *'Frigging Chinese, can't even make a decent cap. If Jimmy Hoffa was still with us, God rest his soul, they'd be buying fortune cookies from us . . . with real fortunes inside instead of all that mumbo jumbo we get from them,'* he muttered.

The enormous expanse of the glass back-patio door slid open and a half-dozen men tumbled out shoving and pushing to get clear. Max spotted Billy Rocket urging them on.

"Find the bastard and bring him to me, don't let him get away," Billy yelled.

Believing that there is truth to the adage that there is safety in numbers, Max fell in with the men and ran around the house, fitting in with the group huffing and puffing. Most of the men ran on wobbly legs and glazed eyes.

"Who we looking for?" he asked in a whisper to a purple haired punk that seemed to be running breathlessly in place, two steps for every one of Max's.

"I'm not sure, man. Billy said find the dude, so we're finding him."

The posse came to a stop at the bedroom window Max had escaped from no more than fifteen minutes ago.

"Now what, dude?" The twin to the pill head next to Max asked.

"I don't know, dude. Billy said it was a cop that broke in and snaked some smack from him. I don't know nothing beyond that except I was smoking some righteous shit when Billy ran through the house yelling and screaming about a cop stealing his stash."

"Maybe Billy just been running to much of his own shit, know what I'm saying?"

"That's what I'm thinking, dude."

Max, always a keen listener saw his way out with the money, "Did he say a cop?" I saw a cop just a little while ago running that way towards the back wall over there. They're heading for the mangroves for sure. Dirty bastards had bundles of shit inside their shirts running and laughing like a couple of fat men, let's get 'em."

"Yeah, let's do this," the twin yelled.

The race to the wall was on, Max laughed as he watched the dumb butts slipping and sliding across the rain soaked lawn. He stuck his head inside the bedroom and threw a leg over the sill. He was half in and half out when cold steel touched the side of his head.

"Nice costume you're wearing, Cabby. A little loose in the crotch, but nice never the less."

"Hey, Billy, what's up?" Max's brain was on hyper speed.

"You're what's up, Cabby, tumble on in, let's talk."

"Sure, Mister Rocket, whatever you say. I came out to jam with you. I was going to call from the gate to give you a heads up, but the rent a cop at the gate waved me through. No shit, Billy, that guy needs to be fired, waving people through like that without a phone call."

"Shut up. What are you doing in my outfit? You look ridiculous."

"No shit, I think so too. That redhead with the funky tongue made me put it on, I swear, Billy. I was minding my own business playing rope-a-dope with Red on the floor over there when the door opened and in walks a guy that looked like Sheriff Polk. I knew in a heartbeat he didn't belong here. Me and Polk go way back, he don't like me and I don't like him. So, I tell Red to roll off, so I could see better, the broad weighs a ton with those big tits and all, know what I mean . . ."

"Where's Janice now?"

"Janice? Oh, you mean Red? Hell, I don't know. When I shoved her off me she grabbed her clothes and left. I mean I was finished, I lost my lust when I saw Polk go into the closet. She called me a prick, can you imagine her calling *me* a prick, *me*? I get thank you letters . . . frigging broad."

"Say another word and I'll cut your pecker off. Janice is my wife, you asshole."

"Your wife! Damn, Billy, I didn't know. She never said nothing or I would have passed. She showed me those tits and the rest is history, man . . ."

Billy tapped Max on the forehead with the pistol.

"You're really pissing me off, dude."

"Ouch! Damn, Billy, that hurt. I was just watching out for you, swear to God." Max was thinking fast. "You can't handle the truth, that ain't on me. I'm just telling you what I saw. The cop pushed the clothes aside and disappeared through a secret door. I thought I would learn more from where I was under the bed, so I hung back."

"Was there a chick on the bed when you came in?"

"A chick . . . on the bed . . . uh . . . when I came in? I don't remember seeing any chick on the bed. I mean there might have been, but I don't remember seeing a chick. I had my hands full with . . . was she blonde?"

"Never mind. Tell me what happened. What did you see?"

"Well . . . he came out with a boo-coo load of smack, stuffing it inside his shirt as fast as he could." Max was gaining confidence, as the lie came together in his pea brain. "He went to the door and must have seen someone coming because he backtracked across the room, gun out and all. I started to reach out and trip him. I could have been on him in a second. A couple of Tai Chi chops and he would have been mine, but I thought it would be better for you if I watched to see where he was going and who his accessories were."

"You mean accomplices don't you," Billy cross-examined.

"Yeah, them guys that help somebody in the act of a crime."

"Maybe I was wrong about you. Get up, let's go out to the kitchen and share a line, man. Your story doesn't make shit for sense, but there's been strange doing around here ever since we got back from the Who Doo Tour"

"Damn, Billy was you fronting for the Stones?"

"Billy Rocket doesn't front for anybody. The Stones are so yesterday, man, I wouldn't even let them front for my front acts. Now, you want a line or what?"

"Geez, Billy, that's generous. What about the guys chasing Polk. Should we check on them?"

"Fuck 'em, they're a bunch of losers anyway. You think a bunch of smack heads are really going to bring a cop down? Really? None of those guys are worth anything except playing backup for me. Hell, Cabby, I *am* the Band. Besides I own Polk. Without him I sure wouldn't be down here in mosquitoville with all these looser rednecks. He earns his pay, believe me."

"Yeah? What ya mean, Billy. What's he do for you, fix traffic tickets for you, maybe tell the neighbors to shut their yaps if the music gets too loud." Max had his radar out. This was big, real big. This could make him one of the guys forever. Jackie would maybe make him a partner in the Sand Bar or even skipper of the *Queen*. Fat chance of that, not with that bucket of guts Bull aboard as captain. He would be the first to be beached if it was up to him. "I'll bet you got Pokey Man by the nuts good and tight, huh, Billy."

"I own the dude. You see those two grunts at the front gate when you pulled in? I snap my fingers and they woof. One time they even delivered the stuff to me when Marcus and Bones were anchored up waiting for the customs agents to come aboard and clear them. They whizzed out on the bight where the *Lucky Lady* was, picked the shit up, and *BOOM*, back ashore before you could say, 'Bob's your uncle'."

"No shit, on the Key West Bight? Man, that takes balls Billy. The customs people that work the bight are tough. I've seen them take a man's boat for just bringing in prescription pills. I remember they had some screwy name for 'em and made a big deal about it. All the suits from Tallahassee were down on the docks like they made the bust themselves, even pushed the guys that made the arrest aside."

"Yeah, if I lost that load, I would have been out a couple million on the tour."

"Damn, a couple million, you're talking some real cash. I knew a guy in Rikers that killed his momma over a million bucks. She ratted him out over some kind of deal that went wrong. He had a couple of Louie V's, not knock offs neither, they were the real deal, stuffed with a million U.S. stacked inside. His momma found them in his closet and called the cops. The dude shot her before the cops got there. To me, I would say the bitch earned it, but that's just me."

Billy stopped cutting lines and looked at Max, "You were in Rikers? Damn, you're a standup guy. What's your real name. I know it's not Cabby."

"Simms, Max Simms. My friends call me Max, everyone else calls me Mister Simms. You can call me Max, Billy."

They shook hands and made a buddy bump.

"Max, guys like you are hard to find. What were you in the joint for, murder, robbery, rape?"

Max flexed his shoulders, and said, "All of the above, Billy, but I don't like to talk about it. Know what I'm saying?"

"Yeah, man, I know. I've never been to the pen but if I ever go down I want to be in California where Charlie Manson is. Talk about a historical dude."

Max looked at Billy like he was crazy. "You nuts, Billy? He cut a German swasticker thingy on his forehead. Who's going to trust a guy that does that?"

"Max, it's cool. I know you're old school and don't believe in existentialism, but Charlie wrote the book on it. Man, just check out those chicks that killed for him just for a smile. He's some heavy shit, man."

"Billy, that ain't right. Everybody knows you ain't supposed to kill and besides he was in the slam for over fifty years, and died there from what I hear, that's what that *extalinguil* stuff will get you. I hear his broads don't like it either."

"Exta . . . What? You're too much Max." Billy laughed and slapped him on the back. "I like you dude, you want a good paying job, there's always room for a man with your . . . uh, smarts. It's easy money, you just need to work the crowd, move a little powder, collect their money and boom, you get a clean ten percent. What ya say? Travel with me and the band, living large, partying every day. It's a good life."

"Damn, Billy, that's the nicest thing anybody ever said to me. Sure, I'd like a job with you and the band, but right now I got to find a kid that wandered off and get him home."

"What kid? You talking about Mikey, Sheila's little boy? Hell, I just saw him a while ago with Marcus, they were heading down to the boat . . ."

"You know Sheila!" Max said, openmouthed. He was visibly shaking, thinking to himself, *'No f'ing way Billy is a murderer! He's got the world by the balls, why would he kill anyone?'* "You know Sheila?"

"Duh? Everybody knows Sheila, know what I mean. She's like the house punch. She'll do me, she'll do you, she'll doobie-doobie-do."

"Sheila? Are we talking about the same broad that works at the Sand Bar?"

"The very same. Little Mikey's mother. She and Renée both work there, talk about a couple of depraved women. The band love them, they want to take the two of them on the road with us along with a couple of other crazy bitches."

"That ain't going to happen, Billy. I guess you didn't hear the tragic news about Sheila, did ya?"

"What news?" Billy asked Max.

"Some animal cut her up while they were doing the nasty, then left her in the mangroves for the crabs."

"Jeezus, that's horrible. She was just here a couple of days ago. Marcus fed her a few roofies and we partied, know what I mean? Who did it?" Rocket questioned.

Max felt reassured listening and watching Billy's face. He was a good judge of character and knew he wasn't the murderer. His gut had never been wrong before, besides, Billy was a rock star.

"My sources tell me that it was Jack Marsh, but I don't believe it. Jack wouldn't hurt a dame, he doesn't need to. The man has more women throwing themselves at him than ten men. Back in the day I had the same problem, but today not so much, but I can spot the curse. It's a burden having dames all over you." Max spun his tale.

"Don't I know it," Billy commiserated. "Sometimes I just want to have a little space without a bunch of crazy bitches pulling on me."

"Hey, Billy, I'm enjoying the yak, but I got to get the kid back to town. Coco's going to have my ass for sure. She's probably screaming bloody murder with that mutt boyfriend of hers up in Miami."

"Not smart, Max. You and the kid better stay here with me until we find out what's going down. I've met her and Marsh both, they're always sticking their noses into other people's business. You stay here where it's safe. I'll send Bones into town to snoop around."

"But what about Renée, I got her out in the cab. I think she needs medical help."

"Don't worry, she'll be fine, some of the boys got a little carried away. She needs to sleep for a while is all."

"I don't know, Billy. I ain't no medic, but she was barely breathing a while ago."

"I said she'll be fine. Now, shut the fuck up and do as I say!"

Max backed off immediately, "Sure Billy, whatever you say. I was just trying to be helpful. You know best for sure. What do I know, I'm a hack driver."

"That's better. Always do as I say, and I'll take care of you. Cross me and I'll put a couple of my heavies, Marcus or Bones on your cabbie ass."

"Sure, Billy. I got it. I'm a good cook, want me to cook up some food for the guys."

"I want you to get Renée out of the cab and down to the boat. Tell Marcus that you, Mikey and Renée are to stay aboard until I find out what is going on. If Marsh killed Sheila, then I don't want Mikey or Renée anywhere close to him."

"Damn straight, Billy. But what about Polk? What if it wasn't him I saw, maybe it was that fat guard at the gate that hit your counting room." Max was thinking fast about the flimsy lie he had thrown out a few moments ago. He needed to create doubt in his cover story. "I'd put money on that's who it was, yeah, that's right, I saw a big black dude come out of that closet, it wasn't Polk . . .."

"No shit, I know it wasn't Polk. I told the boys that to get them out of the house while I took care of Spanky and that asshole James. I've suspected they've being lowballing the count for months. We've been moving more shit every concert, but the money never matched up."

"Wha . . . what ya mean you took care of them? Ya mean like," he slashed his hand across his throat.

"Nah, I had Bones drive them over to the airport and put them on a plane to New York. They're black balled from ever working for anyone in the business again."

"Jeez, Billy, I'll bet that'll give them the squirts, getting fired by Billy Rocket is like, worse than being screwed by Michael Jackson," he laughed nervously.

"Yeah, something like that. You don't fuck with the Rocket Man."

Chapter 14

What had been a seasonal low stalled over the Lower Keys had picked up steam and became a tropical storm. It sat over the islands and spun, forecasters predicted movement to the north within the next twelve hours at five knots and possibly building into a Cat One Hurricane. On Key West, thunder roared through Old Town shaking tin roofs and windows, palm fronds whirled crazily as they beat the air appearing as ghostly aberrations caught in some ancient Voodoo dance. Buttress roots from ancient banyan trees shown reptilian in the slanting rain with every mega explosion of lightning. The uneven sidewalks and potholed back streets popped a ghostly neon indigo with each kiloton flash. Ozone cut the foul-smelling wind carrying a mix of fishy salty air and rotted vegetation. The locals hunkered down with a nose to the wind and a keen ear tuned for trouble. News of the murder had flown across Old Town on night wings of fear. No one knew where or when the murderer would strike again. Murder was no stranger to the town, none the less, the fear of it was carried deep in the hearts of many that rubbed at amulet's and juju's in lamplit rooms.

Electrical power was out on the island making it even more treacherous for Jinx and Judge Powers to maneuver the motor scooter through the backstreets and alleys to the Sand Bar. From Madge's house across from the cemetery on Angela Street to the Sand Bar was less than a mile and should have taken fifteen minutes to get there, but with the storm winds and sheets of rain it was taking them much longer

Jinx hung onto Madge's waist as she maneuvered around limbs and fronds. She dodged rolling trash cans in her path, kicking at one to avert a T-bone hit.

"You're going to kill us on this damn beast of yours, stop with the bumper cars." Jinx hollered in her ear. "Pull over and let me off."

"Hold on, we're almost there," she yelled back at him.

Madge wiped at her eyes with the back of her hand just as a wet scraggly dog ran across her path. She gripped the brake tight causing the motor scooter to fishtail. She regained control and whizzed by the frightened dog.

"Dammit, Madge, that's it. I'm reporting you to Sheriff Polk as unfit to drive. I can't allow you to be running the streets on this damn thing, you're going to kill someone. I can see you on the stand in an orange jumpsuit trying to plea bargain your way out of it . . ."

"Shut up, Jinx. I can't concentrate with you yammering in my ear."

Ten minutes later, Madge slid in behind the Sand Bar at full throttle, one hand on the gas, the other on the brake, just to scare the crap out of Jinx. He went one way and the scooter another.

"That's it! No more!" he screamed, from where he lay on the coral scrabble. "You tried to kill me. You're worse than your old husband, by God. I'll have none of it."

"Shut up and brush yourself off, you big sissy, your no fun. At least Archie could take a joke."

"Joke? That was totally unnecessary. I could have broken my neck, or worse."

"You big cry baby, we've done crazier things in bed. Now, get up and let's see what this is all about."

Cookie opened the locked door and stood back,

"Don't bring no water in here, I just scrubbed these floors. Shake yourselves off outside . . ."

"How are we supposed to do that, Mister C? It's raining outside here. How are we going to shake it off?" Madge asked.

Cookie pondered that for a moment and waved them in, "Next time use an umbrella. I'll not have my kitchen a mess just 'cuz white folks don't know how to come in out of the rain properly. God's truth."

Coco came in from the bar to see what the ruckus was about.

"Thank God, you're both here. So much is happening, I don't even know where to begin," she said.

"Slow down, honey, let's get a drink and you can tell us everything," Madge comforted.

The only light was from a couple of kerosene lamps spread along the bar top. Light melted into the dark exposing Bulls booted feet and knees propped up on a table, his upper body cloaked in shadows. Lamont was snoring softly at another table. Scarlet sat on a bar stool with her chin propped up in her hands, her eyes were red rimmed from crying.

"Well, this is a lively bunch," Madge said. She kicked the swinging door back open and yelled, "Cookie, put fresh coffee on, and whip up a batch of your beignets. We need to wake these people up."

"We're awake, Judge, we just don't know what to do next," Bull said, from the shadows. A nasty smelling cigar smoke ring followed the comment.

"Put that damn thing out or go stand in the rain and smoke it. It smells like a dead cat," Madge said, disgustedly.

"This isn't your courtroom, Judge, I'll not be told what to do." Bull's feet hit the deck with a thud. "I'm tired, I need a shave, I haven't had a good BM in days, and I don't need any advice on where to smoke. Especially, from a judge who wouldn't grant bail to my friend, Jack Marsh!"

"You two break it up. We need to stay focused and not worry about where to smoke a cigar," Coco fumed. "Chief, put out that damned cigar out like the judge said. It stinks awful."

Lamont broke into a hacking cough falling to the floor in a ball retching, "I'm dying. Second-hand dead cat is killing me," he moaned, with a big grin on his mug.

"All right, all ready, I'll put it out. Sheesh, back in the day a man smoked wherever he damned well pleased . . ."

"Back in the day, I would have told you the same thing, that nasty thing stinks." Madge said, holding her nose.

Scarlet fanned a menu in giant sweeps, "The judge is right, Bull, that smell is awful."

Coco and Bull took turns updating Jinx and the judge about what had happened in the last eighteen hours. Coco cried about Renée missing from her apartment and not showing up for work and how Max was afraid to bring Mikey to the Sand Bar because he said the murderer was here, it was someone among us that killed Sheila. Now, Max and Mikey both were missing, holed up somewhere with his phone turned off.

The judge paced back and forth listening as Bull told of following the deputy's car up to Florida City then turning a shackled Jack over to state prison guards at the Everglades Correctional Facility.

"What is Sheriff Polk up to?" The judge asked quizzically, not expecting an answer.

"It has to go back to the shooting of Deputy Kilpatrick, I'm sure. Polk has been convinced that Jack shot the deputy even though he wasn't even in the same part of the warehouse when it happened. It still isn't known who shot Jack. I'd put money on Polk being the shooter. Jack knows who killed Kilpatrick, but he won't talk about it. My money is on Polk being the shooter. Polk was inside the warehouse, it was dark, the gunfire had died off, the Cuban's were all down when the last two shots were fired. There's been bad blood between them for years," Chief Bull said.

"Why the bad blood?" Madge asked.

Coco bit her lower in thought then spoke up, "It goes back years when Jack first arrived in Key West. He had just taken over the Sand Bar and had put most of his money into it when Polk, at that time was a city cop, came around and demanded five hundred dollars a week from Jack to not have any trouble with deliveries and licensing. Jack told him that he would never pay protection money and if he ever came back around asking for it, or caused any trouble, he would beat the hell out of him."

Coco took a sip of water and continued, "A few weeks later Jack was in the kitchen early one morning and heard noise out back and went to see what was being delivered. He never shared what he saw that morning with anyone, then one night we were closing, and Jack called me over to his chair at the bar. He said that if anything ever happened to him that I should tell Bill Price at the Florida Bureau of Investigation what he had seen that morning. Tell him, Polk and his partner, Patrolman Kilpatrick were lifting a limp body into the dumpster. Jack said he was shocked when Polk saw that he had been seen and said, raising his finger to his lips, "You ever tell anyone what you saw, and you'll be a dead man. They shoved the body over the top, dropped the lid and got back into the squad car. As they drove off, Kilpatrick made a finger gun and pointed it at Jack."

"Did Jack tell you this?" The judge questioned her.

"Yes, ma'am, he did. He grabbed my hand tight and swore me to secrecy. He said if anything ever happened to him I should go to the Key West District

Attorney with the story, then to get out of town until things blew over."

"Damn, Coco, why didn't you tell us this sooner. This explains everything. Now we know why Polk hated Jack," Jinx said.

"He actually didn't hate him, he feared him. Polk knew that Jack could come out with the story and Polk's career would be over. Polk and Kilpatrick could be charged with murder, manslaughter, and a dozen other counts," Madge added, thoughtfully.

"The way I see it," Lamont spoke up, "That's why Polk killed Kilpatrick that night and then shot Jack too. Kill two birds with one stone. No more witnesses."

"Exactly, Lamont. My take on it, too." Madge said.

"Ain't nothing, Mizz Judge. I know the criminal mind, having been one myself," he beamed.

"Yes, I could see how you would pick up on the subtleties, young man. Perhaps you can give us more insight on what the criminal mind might be thinking at this point."

"Yes, ma'am, that's easy. Sheriff Polk got Jack under his control and knows this is his best chance to put him down for good, maybe a shiv across the throat by another prisoner, or suicide in his cell, some shit like that . . ."

"Watch your mouth, young man. I won't stand for it."

"Yes'm, I apologize, I was just talking what I know is all. You can't be calling me out for what I don't know, I never made it to judge school, I only went to fifth grade then they sent me off to juvie for killing my momma's boyfriend. After that, I was too busy trying to just get by to worry about if shit or fuck was bad words. In prison, those boys ain't very polite and if they think you're a sissie, they'll cut you up."

Madge looked at him closely and waved him to her. She pulled him in close and hugged him, "Sometimes I forget how cruel the world can be, Lamont. I just see so much of those that never had a chance in life and I've hardened myself to it. I'm sorry, Lamont, I was wrong to call you out."

She wiped at her eyes with the back of her hand which started Lamont to bawling, "That's okay, Mizz Judge, you can't help it, you was just born in a different world than me. Just like I'll never understand them Latino words ya'll speak when you're throwing us poor folk in the slam, shit like *heinous corpses* and such. I figure when they start throwing them kind of words around, my ass is done for."

Madge stopped sniveling and pulled back, looking to see if she was being toyed with. When she saw that Lamont was sincere she pulled him close again and laughed.

"Well, damn, Lamont, I guess I better brush up on my Latino before I go into court again."

Chief shook his head laughing. "Okay you two, enough of the kumbaya, let's stay focused. Jack's in deep trouble, if we follow through with Lamont's thinking then it clears up why Polk sent Jack to the Everglades unit. It puts Jack in the hands of the toughest prison unit in Florida's system where he can just disappear, and no one will ever know what happened to him and it would have happened out of his jurisdiction."

"What do we know about the prison up there, Madge?" Bull asked the judge.

"It's crammed tight with the dregs of the system, recidivists, lifers without parole, rapists, murderers, men that know they are going to die in prison and act that way. The ACLU has been trying for years to have the unit closed with no results. The Florida Attorney General, and the Florida Governor and the Federal Bureau of Prisons ignore any challenges for change. I know there hasn't been an accurate headcount in years other than for the incoming count kept by the Prison Bureau in Tallahassee. Periodically, a list will be issued but it never tallies with the incoming chain list. When asked about a prisoner the answer is always the same, 'No record of receiving said prisoner'."

Jinx helped himself to a bottle of scotch from one of the drink wells and sloshed it into a tumbler, "Why hasn't something been done about this? You would think that the Department of Justice. would jump on this, especially with that powder puff Attorney General we have now. Hell, if it were up to him he would close down all the prisons in the country and let the inmates run the asylum."

"You'd think, but the federal prison system is worse than most states," Madge said, grabbing the drink from Jinx and tossing down half of it."

"Everybody that ever did time inside knows what goes down at that unit. They call it doing *'Island Time'*. They ship your ass down there, they have secret camps out in the swamp where they work a man to death and leave him for the gators. Your ass sent down there, your ass ain't coming back," Lamont said, matter of fact.

"Is that what they say, Lamont?" Madge asked.

"Yes, ma'am. *'In the Yard'*, people talk about the wickedest thing that can happen to a man is to be sent to Florida City for *'Island Time'* or be in one of Louisiana's Atchafalaya camps. Mmm-mm, if the gators don't kill ya, the guards will."

The gathering fell silent in thought. Horrific images of ragged prisoners of war being bayonetted along jungle roads flashed in Bull's mind as Coco thought of whole families disappearing in the dark of Haitian nights never to be seen again.

Coco finally broke the spell, "Oh, my God, Jack could be dead for all we know. His body left out in the swamp for the alligators," she cried.

"Don't jump to conclusions, Honey, Jack's tough, he's not going down that easy," Bull soothed.

"Maybe so, he may be tough, but I think we need to move fast to get him out of wherever he is," Madge said.

Madge searched her cell phone, found the number and called.

"Monroe County Sheriff's office," a sleepy voice answered.

"This is Judge Powers, connect me with Sheriff Polk."

"Uh, Judge, the sheriff is off duty until 0700, it's currently 0130 hours."

"Give me his contact number then," she demanded.

"Uh, no can do, Judge Powers. Policy doesn't allow me to do that."

"Young man, I am a Judge of Monroe County, if I say I want to speak to Sheriff Polk, I expect to be put through."

"Yes, ma'am, but I have my orders. I'm sure that Sheriff Polk will take your call any time after 0700."

"Let's try this a different way then. I'll be over at the jail in twenty minutes, have Jack Marsh cleaned and released by the time I get there. Is that clear?"

"Uh, yes ma'am, it's clear but I can't do that."

"Young man, if you want to keep your badge I suggest you do as I say. I want Mister Marsh released from custody in the next twenty minutes or you'll be policing up Mallory Square each night for the rest of your career."

"Yes, ma'am, but I can't, because he is not at this facility at this time."

Madge winked at the others surrounding her, and continued, "What do you mean he is not at that facility. If not there, where the hell is he?"

"Uh, ma'am, I would prefer that you ask Sheriff Polk about that. All I know is that he was transferred to a different facility at the convenience of the county."

"And just what the hell does that mean, the convenience of the county?" Madge's voice had risen in indignation.

"Yes, ma'am, we've had to shuffle prisoners around because of space limitations. Ever since the city approved that tent city our arrests have quadrupled . . ."

"You don't need to tell me about the vagrancy rates, deputy. I'm the one sending them over to you.

However, I would expect a homeless person to be transferred, not a citizen of the city."

"Yes, ma'am, you would think so, but that's not my decision, Your Honor."

"Where is he then? Marathon? Big Pine?"

"I'm sorry ma'am I'm not allowed to give that information out, Sheriff's orders."

"That cuts it, deputy. I am ordering you to tell me where Mister Marsh was transferred. You have five seconds and then your ass will be unemployed."

"Yes, ma'am . . . I understand . . . but, I'm a union member and you can't be threaten' . . ." The phone went dead.

"Union, my butt, I want his testicles," Madge fumed. "Bull, run me over to Sheriff Polk's house. I'll yank his ass out of bed and we'll get to the bottom of this."

"Madge calm down, for Christ's sake. We know where Jack is, why are we wasting time with Polk? Let's drive up to Florida City and demand his release."

Madge shook her head sadly, and said, "Jinx, we are both officers of the law, we both know that we just can't jump from one jurisdiction to another. If we try and get Jack released from a Florida State facility we to need to go to the state AG and in order to do that we better have our bases covered. Now, get over to the men's room and splash some water on your face. For God's sake, you look worse than some of the bums over in Key West Tent City."

"I want to go along," Coco said.

"Me, too," Lamont threw in.

"No one is going but Jinx and myself, Bull will drive and wait out front. I don't want Polk to see any of you."

"I was thinking the same thing," Bull said. "If Polk suspects that we know what he did, all bets are off. There is no telling what he'll do. We could all be in danger," Bull paused in thought, "My guess is that he won't be working alone either, if he had Kilpatrick as his accomplice before you can bet he will have his rear-end covered with someone else now. He'll have a fall guy, for sure."

"I don't like where this is going," Jinx said, his face furrowed with worry.

"The first place he'll think of will be the Sand Bar. If he feels cornered, he'll hit fast." Bull said. "There's no telling how many men he has loyal to him."

"You may be right, Bull," Madge said. "If he would kill his own deputy to cover up a crime then he wouldn't hesitate to do the same to Jack or any of us. I've rethought this, we need to close the bar and move everyone aboard the *Island Queen* for safety. If anything bad starts to happen, you can just motor out of the bay."

"I like that. I would feel better knowing that Coco and Scarlet are safe." Bull glanced at the two women.

Scarlet had remained quiet, listening to the discussion nervously biting a nail. Bull noticed she started to speak up a couple of times, but let it slide.

"Yo, what about me?" Lamont pointed a finger in his chest. "Those good old boys don't believe in *'Black Lives Mattering'*, uh-uh, not for one second. They'd have my black booty sliced and diced before the screen door slammed. I'm going with all y'all, and that's a fact."

"Of course, you are, and Cookie too." Madge said. "Jinx, you go with them. I'll borrow Bull's pickup and go alone, he wouldn't dare hurt me. He might not feel intimidated if it's just me. If you're along it could get ugly, there's certainly no love lost."

"I need to go with you, Your Honor, you wouldn't stand a chance against him," Bull said.

"No, it's decided, I'll go alone. You get everyone safely aboard the *Queen* and wait one hour for me to return. If I'm not back in an hour, call Bill Price with Florida's Bureau and tell him everything. Coco, we all know you know Bill, don't you?"

"We're very close, um . . . friends, Judge. I was thinking about calling him regardless. I can't take any chances of this getting more out of control. I was waiting until morning to call. He's not going to like that I waited this long, even though he and Jack have their differences, they still have a deep respect for each other."

Scarlet let out a cry of anguish and sobbed, "Miss Duvalier, I think I know where Renée is."

"What! Where?" All heads swung to see Scarlet sobbing into a napkin.

"We didn't want you to know about what we were doing, it was just partying is all," she cried.

"What are you talking about, Scarlet? Stop crying and tell me what you're talking about. Where's Renée?" Coco demanded.

"Sheila met one of the guys that plays in Billy Rocket's band and we all started going there after work to party, you know, drinking and dancing."

"Where is there?" Coco demanded.

"Shark Key," Jinx answered. "Remember yesterday Max was telling us about taking a fare out to Shark Key where he met his idol, Billy Rocket. He was thrilled at having met the man in person."

"I don't know anything about that, but I know that Sheila was getting involved with Marcus, one of the guys in the band. Miss Coco, we know your rule about drugs and we were afraid to say anything. Marcus, one of Rocket's boys was giving Sheila a lot of coke and they would go off by themselves while Renée and I stayed together . . . mostly."

"Did the two of you go there last night after work?"

"Yes, ma'am. I left early because I had to open here at the bar with Lamont. I wanted her to leave with me, but she refused. She hit the coke hard and was all over Billy. I can't stand him, he is such an arrogant ass. He would grab any girl he wanted and drag her off to his bedroom. He called it his magic carpet. That was all bullshit, once he got a girl in there he would shoot her up and do all kinds of freaky things to her."

"Did you ever go with him?"

"No, ma'am, I would never let anyone stick a needle in me, and I sure wouldn't do some of the things some of the other girls did. I was there for the party. I'll admit I did coke, my God, there were punch bowls filled with the stuff, how could I not?"

"Well, another piece of the puzzle falls into place," Jinx said, as he topped off his tumbler from the bottle.

"Lay off the sauce, Counselor, we need to be on our toes. We can't underestimate any of these people," Madge said.

"I'm not drinking to dull my senses, Mad Madge. Rather, I am drinking for courage in the upcoming melee."

Cookie had joined the group and had stood listening quietly, "Y'all give me fifteen minutes and I'll throw together some sammiches and jars of gumbo to take with us. I got some Key Lime pies still left over, probably a few of them coconut pies too in the cooler. It'll only take me a minute. Lord knows how long this storm's going to rage and if we have to scoot down to dem' islands, we're going to need our strength."

"That's not necessary Mister C. The *Queen's* well stocked," Chief Bull said.

"Don't matter, some folks rather have sammiches and pies to nibble on without a big to do."

"Get to it then, we have to move."

Chapter 15

The rain came in fast, one minute the night was heavy with humidity and biting insects the next it was a wall of water. It splashed down on the naked men bringing a moments respite to their aching and tortured bodies. Fat drops of water hammered the hut's tin roof drowning out the night. Rivulets of water snaked down Jack's legs and torso washing away the excrement. The relief was almost orgasmic as the unseen insects washed away with the filth. He steadied himself with his swollen finger tips and bent his head forward to quench his thirst. Water had never tasted so good. It filled his parched mouth and throat as he gulped it down. The liquid brought relief to the cuts and abrasions around his eyes and nose, drowning the pests that had been feasting on the festering wounds. The storm was a miracle, he wasn't sure if he could make it through the night without losing his mind.

Suddenly, hands were on him, grabbing him tight, pulling at him. Jack opened an eye and tried to swing away. The prisoner hanging next to him grabbed fists full of flesh as he climbed up Jack's aching body. The added weight of the other man tore at his legs and joints, the pain was maddening. Flesh that had been deprived of blood flow stung like a thousand wasps as the man continued to climb. Then the pain was gone. He watched as the man pulled himself up on the cross bar and began to untie the nylon line that had held him suspended. Once freed, he pulled the prisoner next to him up enough to bring slack to the line and untied it, letting the man fall to the ground. The man lay writhing in agony as fresh blood pumped through his body.

Jack felt himself swing free as he was lifted a few inches, a moment later he fell into the puddled water below him. He screamed in pain, his body seemed to explode into a million pinpricks as fresh blood ran down from his head and chest to his lower extremities. Muscle cramps twisted him into a ball of fire. A hand covered his mouth cutting off the screams.

"Hush, you going to wake Boss Dalton and then we's all dead."

Jack obeyed the voice, letting the pain roll through his body. The hand disappeared into the night, a moment later a scream of pain came from the fourth man that had been suspended and just as quickly was cut off.

The voice was back.

"I'm leaving, you can come with me or you can stay, makes no never mind to me. If you go with me we'll be moving fast and I ain't stopping until I'm in Mexico, that's for God damn sure. Let's go."

A bright light shown from the porch freezing them in place.

"What y'all doing? Who cut you boys down? I'll have the whole bunch of you in the cage for a month," Boss Dalton bellowed out. "Mister Toby, we got us some runners here."

Like a flash, the big man next to him reached the porch in three giant steps, bounced up the steps and smashed a huge fist into Dalton's face. Dalton dropped like a side of beef, tumbling down the steps into the mud. The man leaped on him, put an arm around his neck and twisted with the other killing him instantly.

"What y'all doing?" Mister Toby hollered. "Get away from that porch."

Toby came out of the dark, slapping a truncheon in the palm of his hand. Next to him was Mister Goodbar swinging a flashlight from Boss Dalton in the mud, over to Jack and the other two prisoners lying in the mud, then back at Dalton and his killer.

"You boys gone crazy, there's going to be hell to pay all around."

"Fuck you, Toby. You ain't no better than this man here," he kicked Dalton.

"Luther, you messed up big time, now get on the ground and let me cage you up before somebody comes down that road and kills us all."

"No way, I'm gone. You want to try and stop me, bring it now, but I ain't spending another minute in this evil place."

"You alive ain't you? As long as you follow the rules you'll stay alive. Like what you done here, though, is going to bring trouble to all of us. You know I got to stop you."

"Yeah, like you helped that redbone you brought in yesterday. I saw them carry him off after Boss Dalton had his way with him. Jenkin's and Floyd carried him off in the skiff to feed the gators, I seen 'em with my own eyes. These white folks are evil, Toby and you know it. The only reason you're still alive is because you suck their ass like it was candy."

"Shut up and get on the ground," Toby started forward with raised club.

Jack made his decision, he wasn't spending another minute in this death camp. He stood on wobbly legs and shouted to draw Toby's attention away from Luther. Goodbar swung the flashlight over to see where this new threat was coming from then flashed it back on the porch steps. Luther was gone. A crashing blow came out of the dark and the flashlight fell to the ground. Pounding flesh and grunts followed shadowed figures as they struggled. Jack wrapped his hand around the flashlight's tube and swung with all his strength feeling bone give, he swung for the same spot, but it was gone. He turned to run and tripped over a body landing face down in the mud. He came up spitting and gasping as a giant hand pulled him to his feet.

"Come on, let's *de de mou*, they going to be on us before daybreak. We got to put space between us and them, they'll kill us for sure if they catch us."

Jack didn't have to be told twice, he knew the old Vietnamese words for *'run Jackie run'*, well not the exact translation, but close enough to fit his current situation.

"Not so fast, Luther. Drag Toby and Goodbar over to the porch, I'll be right back."

Dozens of eyes watched Jack from the shadows of the prisoner huts as he made his way up the steps and entered the hut. No prisoner had ever gone up those steps uninvited. Inside, Jack hurried through the two rooms, he found what he was looking for hanging from a wall peg, a holster holding a .357 and another with a 9mm automatic. He pulled a pair of trousers off a third peg and slipped them on, next came the shirt with the badge and shoulder patches. The bedsheet was wadded and thrown on the floor, two pillows were blood stained, and a half bottle of whiskey sat on the nightstand. Jack took a healthy swig and gargled deep and spit it on the mattress. The shock of the alcohol on his cut mouth staggered him. He tore off a swath of sheet and soaked it with the remainder of the whiskey then daubed at the deep cuts around his eyes. He screamed in agony and fell back on the bed. It took a moment before he could catch his breath, fresh blood oozed out of the deeper cuts.

Back on the porch he slid around into the Nine's chamber and shot Toby in the throat. A gasp went up from the onlookers, even Luther stepped back at the unexpected action. Jack chambered another round and fired it into Goodbar's neck. He put the pistol in Boss Dalton's hand after wiping if down with the shirttail, making sure that lots of Dalton's blood smeared it. Again, without hesitating, he shot Dalton in the chest from a few feet away. He placed the .357 in Toby's big hand and pulled a fat finger through the trigger guard then let the hand fall into the growing bloody mud puddle circling the three dead men.

"You are one crazy dude," Luther said, still in shock at what he had just witnessed.

"Not really, just covering our ass. Let's roll."

Luther led the way out of the camp, all eyes followed them in silent confusion until the rain swallowed them up then chaos broke out. Men ran into the hut screaming and yelling obscenities, tearing apart everything they could get their hands on, others tore through the mess tent pulling canned goods and food items from the pantry, while even others disappeared into the swamps.

Luther signaled for Jack to wait there and he disappeared into the rain. A moment later he was back pulling a narrow swamp skiff on a line.

"It doesn't have a motor, but it'll keep us out of the water and away from the gators. Hop in, and I'll put some distance between us and this shit hole."

Jack sat in the bow of the skiff peering ahead into the rain as Luther poled them forward. They would glance off a mangrove root or bottom out and he would pole around it.

"How do you know where we're going?"

"I don't, I'm just going by the noise fading behind us. Hell, we might be going in circles for all I know," Luther admitted.

"Great. We kill three people and make the great escape into gator infested swamps and we have no idea where we are or where we are going."

"Stop complaining, we're alive aren't we. Once the sun comes up, we'll head south for Florida Bay . . . maybe."

Chapter 16

The aroma of bubbling gumbo on the galley burner filled the main cabin with mouthwatering anticipation.

The ride over stuffed in Bull's crew cab wasn't bad until Jinx belched a cloud of ninety proof. Bull had finally had it and pulled to the curb and insisted Jinx ride back in the bed the rest of the way over to the *Queen*.

Jinx was half in the bag and became belligerent, demanding that the women should ride in the back, as was there due. The rest of the short ride was spent, the females in glaring silence.

Once aboard, Scarlet curled up in one of the stuffed chairs in the main cabin and continued to cry, Jinx stood on the aft deck under the awning watching as Madge disappeared down Eaton Street heading for Sheriff Polk's house on Stock Island. Bull and Coco were on the bridge listening to the police scanner for any tidbits that they could glean.

Lamont was harassing Cookie in the galley about the pros and cons of being a black man in a white man's world.

"Lamont, you just putting yourself into a tizzy tail worrying about that nonsense. There ain't nothing you can do about that. Jesus blessed us long before he blessed them white men."

"That's nonsense, Mister C. We been black forever."

"That's what I'm saying, He blessed us back before the flood, before the garden even, He saw us and called us His creation back when the onliest ones of us was black."

"You believe that trash?"

"Sho' do, they been riding our coattails all this time. You learn to hold your head high, Lamont, besides, the good Lord ain't got no color. He don't see nothing but our goodness."

Madge had pulled down the single lane road fronting Polk's raised cinderblock house and parked. The front yard was a large square of crushed corral with his Sheriff's car parked between a trailered flats boat on one side and a new Humvee on the other side. Stacked lobster traps filled the space beneath the house. Polk's wife left him and their small son years before for a personal injury lawyer from Miami. At the time, the breakup almost cost Polk his bid for Key West's Monroe County Sheriff, but he managed to dodge that bullet by making his wife out to be a tramp that would hit anything that wore pants.

Madge thought Polk was the most disgusting and crude man she had ever met and that he had no place in law enforcement. She also suspected he was dirty just by hearing backchannel gossip and stories whispered. She wondered how he could afford some of the things he wore on a sheriff's salary. She commented once at a cocktail party about the gold Rolex he was wearing and his diamond pinky ring. He ignored her and continued on with their idle chitchat. She wasn't afraid of him in the least, she didn't fear any man, but none the less she hesitated before climbing out of the truck cab. Just for a moment she had misgiving about not bringing Bull or Lamont along with her for moral support or muscle if needed.

The yard lit up bright as she walked across the yard startling her. She gripped the small pistol that she always carried, a gift from her late husband. He had told her that she just needed to pull the trigger a couple of times then run like hell. She tried to steady her trembling hands by taking deep breaths and exhaling slowly as she moved up the stairs.

"Who's there?"

She recognized Polk's voice immediately.

"Judge Powers, Sheriff, we need to talk."

The front door opened outward and Polk's head and bare torso followed, "Talk about what. Can't it wait until morning, I got company here."

"It's important, we need to talk now. Put some damn clothes on and let me in out of this rain."

"Just a minute."

She stood in the rain and waited a few minutes, got tired of waiting and stepped inside the front door. The place was nothing like she had imagined it would be; red velvet wall paper, golden silk drapes held back with ornamental rope tassels, upholstered overstuffed chairs, a loveseat of black crushed velvet. Her first thought was that of a whorehouse or an effeminate man. But certainly not a sheriff in one of the largest counties in the state.

"How dare you come in! I told you to wait, I was putting trousers and a robe on. We can talk down below." Polk was shaken, beyond embarrassed, it was more like being outed. Fear and hate wrinkled his face. "Get out, get out now," he demanded.

A willowy young man came out of the bedroom wearing a tiny thong, He flipped his longish hair, and said, "Poppy, hurry and finish. I want you to come back to bed with me."

Madge stood openmouthed at the scene before her, "Uh, maybe I should come back later, Sheriff. Yes, I think I'll leave now."

"You're not leaving now, get away from the door," Polk commanded, still burning with humiliation. "Armand, put on a robe and fetch Sampson."

"Oooh, a party, I do love a party," Armand sashayed rhythmically, as he disappeared back into the darkened room.

"Don't even think it, Polk. I'm out of here," she said. She remembered the pistol in her hand and raised it. "Don't try to stop me. I know how to use this."

"Why, Judge, I thought you wanted to talk. Now put that pea shooter away and sit here." He motioned to the love seat, his humiliation gone, replaced by hatred.

She ignored his invitation to sit. "Tell me what is so important that you would intrude on my private life."

"It's nothing, really. I couldn't sleep and thought this would be a good time to catch you away from your busy schedule . . ."

"Stop with the bull crap, Madge. Talk to me."

Armand slipped into the kitchen wearing a Pepto-Bismol pink silk robe with a flowing ostrich feather collar and out the backdoor. A moment later Marge heard the muffled growls and snarls of a large dog, then pounding footsteps up the stairs.

She had several cases from the past that were for dog fighting and she threw the book at them, too, but never actually saw a live fight or the dogs pitted against each other, until now. Sampson was unquestionably a fighting dog and bore the scars to prove it. He had a missing eye and part of a badly healed cheek exposing a row of teeth giving him a grizzly appearance. She caught her breath as he lunged at her.

Polk snapped his fingers and pointed to his side. Samson obeyed immediately and fell at his master's feet breathing out of its ugly maw.

"Where were we?" he said. "Oh, yes, you were about to share something with me that couldn't wait until morning."

Madge reluctantly took her eyes off the dog, and said, "I want to know under what authority you moved Jack Marsh out of my jurisdiction and into a state facility."

This seemed to take Polk back for a moment. He had thought she was here to tell him she had rethought her decision to not let Marsh post bail in which case he was prepared to lie and tell her that he had made another attempt on the life of a fellow inmate and would be a flight risk. He didn't know Marsh had been seen being transferred to the Everglades State Unit. The game just went into overtime. He knew he didn't have the authority to transfer an inmate into a state facility without prior approval of a judge, in this case, her.

"You know very well we are way overcrowded, Judge. If the Bureau of Prisons or some touchy-feely group found out we're stacking six men into each two-man cell, there would be all hell to pay."

"I'm aware of that, Sheriff, but if that was the case why not wait until the weekly chain is made up and bus him up there according to normal practice? No, I have it on good authority that you had a deputy drive him yesterday morning alone and released to a guard out in the parking lot of the Everglades Unit. Is that correct protocol?"

Polk's eyes lost focus for a moment. "You don't understand, Judge, Marsh is a dangerous man. He is always sticking his nose in my business. He's a murderer and should be put away for life. His little minions are no better, they do his bidding like trained monkeys, especially that little idiot Max Simms. He defends Marsh like a dog."

Madge, still standing, was regaining her composure, and spoke up, "Sheriff, I have it from a reliable source that you killed Deputy Kilpatrick and then tried to kill Marsh to cover up a crime committed by you and Kilpatrick many years ago, so don't try and throw blame on an innocent man, Sheriff."

Polk sat down in shock. He couldn't believe what he had just heard. No one knew the truth of that night in the warehouse drug bust when he had killed the idiot, Kilpatrick. The bastard was threatening to go to the DA and tell everything unless he got a bigger cut of the drugs, kickbacks, and the money laundering. The bastard had demanded fifty percent of the business. He needed killing, and Marsh was a constant reminder that he could open his yap at any time and blow the whistle on him. He had to go. Now, this bitch knew everything.

The thought of killing a judge hit him with a spike of fear that staggered him. He knew he had crossed the line years ago, but there was a difference in being a dirty cop and a murderer and now the ultimate sin to kill the very essence of what he believed in but never lived, obedience and respect for the law. He had always been above the law, but that bench mark had been set by timid men. His conscience never bothered him dealing in drugs. If some punk dealer or user got killed in the process of a raid, so be it. It was no loss to society, hell, they even handed out medals and promotions, the bigger the bust. What happened to the money and drugs after the twenty-four-hour news cycle moved on was the sweet part. The drugs were moved back to the street and the money to stuffed war chests and numbered accounts.

He bit a knuckle as the solution to closing all of this down and disappearing into the islands congealed. He could live ten lifetimes with the money he had stashed, but first he had to erase all signs off his involvement in any crimes.

"Samson, watch the judge while I get dressed. If she moves, tear her apart."

Madge pulled herself in tight as the dog looked at her as if he understood every word his master had spoken.

"My God, Polk, what are you doing? Have you gone mad?"

"Not hardly, Your Honor. I'm perfectly sane. In fact, at the moment, I am absolutely fucking brilliant."

"Poppy, where are we going with this?" Armand had listened to the exchange and knew instinctively that something bad was afoot. He hadn't survived in Key West by being the silly girl he pretended to be, not hardly. Years of working the streets of Hollywood had taught him how to survive in the shadow world of being gay where straight men would do anything to keep their illicit life secret, even kill.

"Don't worry, my bunny rabbit. You'll be hippity-hopping along in just a few minutes."

Madge stood frozen in place as Polk walked to her and took the pistol from her hand without any resistance. She shivered in fear as Polk slid the chamber back, turned and shot Armand in the forehead. Armand fell dead without a whimper.

Madge screamed at the loud report in the confined space.

"My God! What have you done? You killed him . . . you shot him in the head . . ."

"Shut up!" Polk backhanded her, knocking her to the floor.

He hurried out of the room and was back in a few seconds with bedsheets and towels.

"Clean that mess up and wrap him in the sheets, we're going for a ride."

Madge was too scared not to obey. She quickly knelt and wiped the blood and gore from the tile floor then wrapped the young man's body in a shroud of sheets. She began to cry uncontrollably for Armand and cradled him to her bosom rocking back and forth. She thought of her late husband and the cancer that had eaten him up just as he was beginning to enjoy his retirement from his law practice. She cried for Jinx and prayed that he would someday quall the demons that were riding him into oblivion. But, mostly she cried for herself and for her hardened heart that had become so callous and cynical. She hated herself knowing that she held sway over people's lives by incarcerating their bodies and in some, their souls, that would mark their time on earth. Who was she to have such control? Who was she after all to pass judgement?

"Stop with the blubbering, Judge, we're out of here."

Madge swiped at her nose with her sleeve, and tried to regain her composure.

"Where are we going?" she asked, noticing that he had changed into his uniform and carried a garment bag over his shoulder and a brief case in his other hand.

"You'll see soon enough, here . . . carry these for me," he ordered.

He grabbed Armand's shroud and dragged him across the floor and out the front door. He turned off the porchlight, gave the body a push, and watched it tumble down the stairs. He motioned for Madge to move it, pulled the door tight behind him and followed her down the stairs.

"Give me the keys to this piece of junk," he said, as he grabbed her shoulder bag and dug around until he found what he was looking for.

"Get in . . . and buckle up, we don't want to be stopped and ticketed," he laughed at the absurdity of his joke.

With little effort, he lifted Armand's lifeless body into the back floorboard then slammed the door. A loud crunch cut through the rain.

"Frigging queer," he said, as he bent the mangled leg and slammed the door again.

It took twenty minutes to drive through the rain and flooded streets to get to Madge's house. The hundred-year-old two-story house was shrouded in watery shadows, pockets of darkness seemed to watch as he pulled the body from the pickup letting it fall to the gutter.

"What are you doing, Polk? I don't like what's going on here." Madge struggled, as he pulled her from the cab and spun her around. He expertly cuffed her hands then bent to whisper in her ear.

"I think you'll love the irony of what's going to happen, Your Honor. We're going to hold court where you are the accused, poor Armand, the victim, and me as the judge and jury . . . AAGGGHH!"

Madge kneed him as hard as she could. Polk went down in a ball of fiery pain. She kicked him again and ran. Polk rolled around watching her, his heart was pounding in his chest, his testicles shattered in pain. Fear grabbed him and took over, he stood in a crouch and began running after her.

This was Madge's territory now, she knew it well from jogging the back alleys and streets of old town every morning for years. She ran around her house and down the alley towards Margaret Street, from there it would be a straight shot over to the bight and safety.

Polk sucked up the pain in his crotch and chased Madge's fleeing shadow into the alley. He knew he couldn't let her get away, that would screw up everything. He had plans, and they didn't include spending the rest of his life in the slam. The bitch would nail him to the cross if she got away. He turned and ran back to the truck, ignored Armand's body and cranked up the pickup. He spun the wheel around and goosed the powerful motor, hit the cemetery wall knocking a swath of the ornate brick and wrought iron works down, bounced back and shot forward. At the corner he turned left and spotted a running figure a couple of blocks ahead. In an instant, he was on top of Madge, hitting her and flipping her high into the air. He jammed on the breaks, ran back and picked up her shattered body and tossed it in the bed of the truck. The hour was late, and the street was dark, but he still took a moment to look around for any witnesses. At this point, there was no turning back, one or two more dead wouldn't matter.

Armand's body had floated down the flooded gutter from where Polk had dumped it giving Polk's system a jolt of adrenalin. Two large scruffy street dogs were tugging at the mangled foot. Polk pulled up alongside and shot them with pepper spray. The mongrels yipped and ran off in agony.

"Come to Poppy," he said, as he pulled the soaked body from the gutter and tossed it on top of Madge's body.

It took a couple of minutes to make his way over to Truman Street then head north. The intensity of the storm had picked up, even with the wipers on maximum the outside world was blurred and distorted. At White Street, the hanging stop light hung by one strand of cable swinging wildly, a downed queen palm blocked his lane. As he pulled around the palm, the stop light broadsided the cab with a loud shattering of the driver's side window and door. Millions of little diamond squares of safety glass rained in on him, and instant later the side airbag exploded knocking him aside throwing out a powdery substance filling the cab air. He was blinded for a moment, hit the brakes, and slid off the road hitting the metal light pole with a crunching fender bending noise. He wiped at his eyes, just as a hot transformer crashed into the roof in a detonation of sparks then bounced off into the middle of the street.

Polk cleared one eye and floored the gas pedal, he had to get out of there immediately before some swing shift city cop rolled up. He crossed the bridge onto Stock

Island doing eighty and didn't back off until he passed Murray Marine.

Luck was with him until he turned left onto Shark Key. An oncoming vehicle t-boned the heavy pickup and spun off in a blaze of sparks and screams. The pickup tumbled, throwing Polk clear of the cab into the roadside culvert. The shock of the flowing water acted as a catalyst reviving him almost immediately. He pulled himself up onto the roadside and laid still taking an inventory of his banged-up condition.

The deputies that were assigned by Polk to watch the comings and goings on Shark Key had been dozing when the accident occurred. Both men came out of their stupor in a flash and were on the scene. The woman in the oncoming vehicle was dead, her body twisted among the steel, plastic and glass. One deputy hurried over to a nude man partially wrapped in a sheet, the back of his head gone.

"What the hell is this? Roy, check this out. This boy's been shot."

"Throw out some flares, Sarge, we got a woman over hear still alive, barely, but breathing."

"Roger that." The sergeant ran to his patrol car and hit the brilliant light bar across the top of the unit. The flashing blue and white lights lit up the entire intersection. Several cars from both direction had already stopped and came forward.

Unbelievably, Sheriff Polk appeared in the glare waving his hands.

"Get those people back. Keep everyone away from the scene." He ran to the ripped and torn truck reached in and pulled his suitcase and briefcase out by the strap.

"Sergeant Parr, help me get these people into your patrol car right now. I don't want them found here"

"What are you talking about, Sheriff? Two are dead and the lady over there is barely hanging on. We need to get her to the hospital asap."

"Shut up and do as you're told, Parr."

Sergeant Parr ran back to the unit and pulled it alongside the sheriff who was leaning over the body in the sheet.

"Give me a hand, get him in the backseat."

"What about the old lady, she's still alive."

Get her in the back seat, too. I arrested both of them and I need to keep them in sight," Polk lied. "You and your partner work this scene, get it cleaned up and don't put anything in your report about me being here . . . and you never saw these two stiffs."

"But, Sheriff, none of this makes any sense. Where are you going with the unit? What about the old lady, and who was driving the truck? How am I supposed to explain all that?"

"You're a fancy ass sergeant, you figure it out."

Polk got behind the wheel and punched the pedal. The supercharged patrol car shot across the highway and blew by the security gate. Rent-A-Cop Ray Bodine watched in disbelief, as the patrol car disappeared down the street deep into the exclusive residential area.

"Billy Rocket . . . you're mine, you sick fuck."

Chapter 17

Terawatt bolts of lightning exploded in the blackness, igniting the night with grotesque frescos frozen for an instant. Then gone, leaving the sharp smell of ozone thick in the wet air. Thunder ignited with megaton explosions reverberating across the Everglades. Small and large creatures alike burrowed deeper into their lairs not daring to venture out, they would go hungry this night, not willing to chance being taken by a stealthy predator.

The glow off to the left confused Jack, thinking it was the first glow of morning light. It didn't make sense; how could it be morning already.

"Luther, look. Is that daylight."

Luther stopped poling and looked. "That's the camp burning, I'm thinking. Those idiots just want to get caught."

"Yeah, well, I guess we do, too. We've been out here for over an hour and we haven't gotten very far. At this rate we'll be back where we started in no time."

"No, we'll be okay, now that we have something to steer by. We'll keep the fire off our port beam and let it drop off aft to judge our distance. We'll either hit

Alligator Alley to the north, Florida Bay to the south, or somewhere along the west coast."

Jack turned and looked at his companion, "How do you know about navigation, Luther?"

"Ha, you thought I was just some shuck and jive dude off the streets, didn't you? That pisses me off. You probably think I was a gangbanger doing hard time for killing his baby's momma or some cheap drug bust. Listen up, Mister. I graduated from Florida State with an engineering degree, three years ago. I had plans to go into the Army Corps of Engineers, build things, maybe over in the Middle East or Africa. Or better yet, in our own fucked up country. Everywhere you look we need new roads and bridges. If we could harness the power of the billions of gallons of fresh water just below our feet here in our own state of Florida, we could generate enough electricity for a hundred years," he seemed to have gone off into different place.

"As a graduation gift, my parents bought me a new Mustang, red as a firetruck. That baby was running over four-hundred horses that sucked up gas faster than a home coming queen could do a linebacker. Damn, it was fast."

"This going somewhere, Luther? I think we better be thinking about putting distance between us and the bad guys."

"Hear me out, Jack. I want to show you how my life is judged much cheaper than your life. I picked up my girl from her folk's house in Ocala to show her the Beast, that's what I named the Mustang. Silly huh?"

"Not really, I had an Impala back in the day that we called the Roach Coach because it had so many cheeseburger wrappers, jimmy foils, and blunts overflowing all the trays and holders."

"Not mine, it was pristine. Anyway, I roll onto I-75 North and punch it, traffic was light, and I ran her up to a hundred. My girl had the radio blaring and was looking hot as hell beating out the rhythm on the dashboard. I took my eyes off the road for a just a few seconds to check her out and I hit a frigging eighteen-wheeler blown tire in the road. The next thing I know, I wake up in Shands Hospital in Gainesville with a broken leg and arm, and a shitload of staples across the back of my head. A nurse came in, accompanied by a dude in a suit and he begins to read me my rights. He says I was charged with vehicular manslaughter for the death of Mindy Sloan. Once I was able to be transported to a court, I was officially charged and denied bail. The all-white jury found me guilty, the judge hit me with a thirty-five-year slam . . . and the rest is history . . . almost."

"That's a pretty heavy sentence, Luther. What did you do to piss off the judge?"

"I didn't piss off the judge, Jack. She was born pissed off, just like the all-white jurors. They were pissed off, because Mindy was a white girl and I'm as black as their hearts."

"Yeah, well get over it, Luther, life's a bitch. Right now, we need to scoot on down the bayou or the dogs will be on us."

"Yas suh, massa, yas suh. I bees paddling fas' as I can. Da' dawgs be chasing Huck and Jim."

Jack laughed at the comment, and said, "Paddle, Jim, we gots to be in Illinois by daylight, they's after us."

Both men laughed then fell silent. Even through the maelstrom of the storm they heard the dull thump of shotguns being fired way off in the mangroves.

"The devil's out tonight, Jack. If he catches us there won't be any sunrise for us, boy."

A steady bright light swept by missing them by a few yards, the sound of the helicopter was right behind it. Luther bent to his pole as Jack dipped cupped hands on the bow adding to their forward movement. Jack pulled hard, ignoring the unseen little things in the water that resisted their passage. The light was back, Luther lurched forward and tumbled out of the skiff. Water spouts erupted around Jack, a round creased his scalp with an atomic blast of light and pain. He fell forward as molten lava melted consciousness. The whiteout lasted a few seconds then burned off leaving searing pain.

The shooter must have thought he had scored two kills and moved on to the glare of the burning camp. Jack came back to the world slowly then remembered Luther. He twisted around frantically searching the darkness. A bolt of lightning lit up the sky followed by a clap of thunder, lasting long enough for Jack to spot Luther caught in a tangle of mangrove roots. He dove over the side and sank to his waist in the fetid water, his bare feet sank into slimy mud that sent disgusting shivers up his legs. Putrid smelling bubbles broke the surface, the smell making him wretch.

"Luther . . . talk to me," he said, as he pulled the limp body free of the tangle.

Jack couldn't tell if he was alive or not, he ran his hands over the body hunting for an entry or exit wound and found a gaping hole in the lower back.

"Get your hands off me, you sick pervert," Luther mumbled.

Relief flooded Jack. He felt a closeness to this man that had freed him from his bonds and then escaped from the prison camp together into the night after killing three men. Surviving through life and death experiences bonds men together faster than any oath or pledge could ever do.

"Shut up, hold onto my back and I'll get us back aboard the skiff. I think we're just body count for now, but come daylight we better be long gone, they'll be out matching names up with the dead."

Wrestling Luther's deadweight aboard capsized the narrow skiff on the first try, the second was successful, but the pole was gone. Jack splashed around both sides in frustration and finally gave up. He tore a sleeve off Boss Dalton's uniform shirt he was wearing and tied it off to the bow cleat giving him a short painter line to pull.

Jack kept the camp glow at his six o'clock position as he took each cautious step in the dark night, releasing gaseous bubbles from the primordial mud with each shuffled step. He bent to his task pulling the skiff through the swampy water, blood pouring down his face from the scalp wound. Flying insects braved the rain barrage to feast on the unexpected cornucopia. Unseen creatures looked on from their lairs, bewildered by the strange forms out and about on a night such as this, hungry eyes let it pass not sure if it were prey or predator.

After an eternity of muscle aching time, the water reached his chest, then his chin, and he began scissor kicking rather than swallow any of the putrid water. The stagnant water became sluggish then quickly it was flowing. Jack let go of the bow and grabbed the stern as his speed picked up. Using his body as a rudder, he zipped down a wide canopied stream keeping to the center. A weak light shown ahead, a moment later he knew they were safe. Flamingo Marina was on his starboard as the stream widened into a small harbor with a wall of mangrove on the portside. He guided the skiff to the dock, kicking hard against the tidal flow that wanted to pull him out into Florida Bay. He knew where he was. A thirty-three-foot Grady White with twin Mercury 350 4-Stroke engines was tied off at the tip of the dock, rising and falling against its jumper lines. Jack held onto the gunnel and hand-walked his way to the stern then tied off his makeshift painter line to the stair platform. He climbed aboard and checked out the cabin. Satisfied that no one was sacked out below, he went back to the dive platform and manhandled a semiconscious Luther aboard. He gently laid him on a cushioned side bunk then went topside to check for any prying eyes. The dock light was a small solar light that was quickly running out of energy, but still bright enough to spot visitors. Back aboard he found the keys exactly where all boaters kept their keys, in the cup receptacle by the captain's chair. The twins came alive with a growl then fell into a low rumble that couldn't be heard over the storm. Jack made quick work of the bow and jumper lines. Letting the current swing the boat out towards the bay. He let loose the stern line and drifted away from the dock, advancing the throttles to give him headway against the turbulent wind, then once out in the channel he spun the wheel to starboard to follow the narrow channel out, keeping the red markers off the portside. Clear of the markers, he spun the wheel to 180° and pushed the boat up on plane. The twins jumped to the command and flew south, bouncing crazily in the turbulent waters.

Once out in the bay and the land mass was a couple of miles to the stern, he pulled back on the throttle and locked the wheel in place then went below. Luther was on the deck rolling listlessly unconscious from the pain and blood loss. Jack turned on the cabin lights, found the first aid kit in the hatchway locker and dumped the contents on the galley counter. Using his knee, he wedged the big man tight against the cabinet, poured the bottle of alcohol on the gaping wound. Luther came awake with a scream, arching his back as the chemical worked its magic. Jack rummaged through the tubes of unguents and powders and came up with a tube of sulfonamide.

"Hold on, buddy, this shouldn't hurt," he said, as he squeezed the entire tube into the wound. "This is going to kill every little critter within a foot of this hole."

Luther was in distress, he was hot to the touch, and his skin had a gray pallor to it. Jack slathered a gob of antibiotic on a giant wad of compresses then taped it down tight.

"You're going to be fine, we pulled it off, Luther."

Luther nodded without opening his eyes, "Be quick, Jack, I'm feeling weak."

Jack went topside and strapped himself into the captain's chair, took the helm off lock and punched the three-fifties.

Once back up on plane, he snatched the mic from the bulkhead mount, and tuned in the radio to channel 16 . . .

"*Queen, Queen,* come in, over." Static bounced back. "*Queen, Queen,* come in, this is Bravo Six, over."

Jack bent forward to hear better. Nothing but static. He placed the mic back in its cradle and concentrated on holding his course.

"Bravo Six, Bravo Six, this is the *Queen,* over." Bull's voice was tinny and distant.

Jack snatched up the receiver, "*Queen,* Bravo Six."

"Bravo Six, urgent message, go to channel 73. Now. *Queen* out, this channel."

Chapter 18

Polk came to a skidding stop under the portico of Billy Rockets home, emergency light bar twirling in the rain. The guards on duty didn't know to draw down on Polk or not. He was a frequent visitor, but what the hell was this about?

"Sheriff, what's with the Miami Vice entry? Back it down a little . . ."

A purple haired boy came out to see what the commotion was about, and screamed.

"It's him, arrest him. He broke into Billy's room and took all of his sugar." The man ran back in the house, screaming, "*BILLLYYYY*! I found him . . . I found him . . ."

Polk snapped the streetsweeper from the dashboard and cranked a round of double oughts into the chamber, "Back down, Fat Man, or you'll be taco sauce."

"Sure, Sheriff, whatever you say," Fat Man said, shaking, not wanting a beef with this guy who he knew to be very dangerous and unpredictable. Stories of the sheriff and some of the girls, and boys were a little disgusting for his tastes.

"That's better, get some of the boys to help and take the two stiffs in the backseat around to the boat. Billy and I will be along in a few minutes," Polk commanded.

"Stiffs? I don't want no part of this shit, man. I signed on to be muscle for Billy, but I'm not taking a fall for nobody."

"You be on that cell phone in three seconds or you're a dead man. I don't have time for you . . . one . . ."

"Okay, okay." He hit a button and a voice answered. "I'm clearing Sheriff Polk inside to see Billy. I need a couple people out here to help with a couple of, uh . . . stiffs"

"Stiff's," the voice laughed. "Is the dickhead bringing along his own little boys again?"

Sheriff Polk heard the transmission and snatched the phone from Fat Man, "Who is this? Answer me, you fuck." He threw the phone at Fat Man and hurried into the house, yelling over his shoulder. "Get those bodies to the boat, and don't let anyone in or out of the compound until I say so."

Billy was in the counting room bundling up the remaining stacks of banded bills into the plastic tubs, getting ready for it to go aboard the *Lucky Lady*. Usually Marcus and Bones made the cash run to the Cayman where they would cart it down to the Bank of the Netherlands and deposit it or put it into the bank's spacious basement locker for safe keeping. The bank director was more than willing to help Billy in anyway needed since he was allowed to syphon off a cool twelve percent for himself. Later that day, after dropping off the cash, Marcus would make a call to an unlisted number, say a few words, and hang up. An hour later a bakery delivery truck would pull down to the public dock in George Town and unload large tins of baking powder destined for Vera Cruz, Mexico. Once loaded aboard, the truck would drive a way, and the *Lucky Lady* would make way for Key West Bight.

But tonight, Billy was thinking . . . *'it would be good to get away for a week or so, maybe bounce over to Montego Bay for a few days of R&R with the locals after he finished his business in George Town. There was also the trouble with Sheila being dead and Renée OD'd on coke stashed aboard his boat. What was the deal with Mikey, too? What the fuck was he going to do with a kid? Maybe he could turn it into a publicity stunt, maybe* adopt him, like the Hollywood chicks adopting babies from Africa as a PR stunt. Everyone knew that the paparazzi moved on to the next scandal once the baby was passed off to a nanny for the rest of its childhood.'

A pounding on the door brought him out of his thoughts, as he quickly put tops on the large tubs of money. He put an ear to the door and listened, a quick series of slams made him lurch back, 'The Fuck!'

"Who is it?"

"Me, Polk, open up, we have trouble."

Billy slid the locks and bolts back and let Polk into the room, shutting and locking it behind him.

"What are you talking about? What kind of trouble?" Shivers ran up Billy's spine.

Polk appeared to be confused for a moment then the confusion twisted to hate as the image of Jack Marsh appeared. It was Marsh's fault that his world was collapsing, not his own fault. He should have shoved a needle of a nitric acid mix into Marsh while he was unconscious after the beatdown in his cell. It was too late now to kill him with his own hands, but that idiot, Warden Cotton, was doing his dirty work for him, the sadistic bastard. Marsh would be alligator meat within a week and the world will be less one asshole. Meanwhile, he'll be humping some young thing in Barbados or Anguilla, 'Maybe I should ask Cotton for some video of Marsh, postpartum,' he laughed at the image.

"Polk! Polk. Snap out of it. What kind of trouble are we in?" Billy was snapping his fingers in front of the sheriff's face.

"Judge Powers paid me a visit tonight, she knows everything. She knows I framed Jack Marsh, she knows I protect your drug business . . ." His mind was becoming confused about how much the judge had revealed about him and how much she knew about Billy. Oh well, it didn't matter what he told Billy, once they were loaded on the *Lucky Lady,* Billy was going to disappear overboard anyway.

"I don't have any idea of what you're talking about. Have you been snorting to much product?"

Polk laughed, "Never touch your stuff, Billy. It's been cut too many times. I can fly and play sheriff at the same time." He lifted a lid off one of the tubs and whistled. "Some serious change here, partner. I've been thinking a lot about how much product you move on your tours and the cash that comes back. I think it's time we bumped up my piece of the pie."

Alarm bells banged in Billy's ears. Where was this going? He knew that someday Polk would come around for more protection money, but now he had a bad feeling about this whole conversation, there was something wild in Polk's eyes.

"How big of a piece did you have in mind, Sheriff?"

"I'm not greedy, they say *'don't kill the goose that lays the golden egg'* and we certainly don't want to do that. I'm thinking we go full partnership, do a fifty-fifty split."

Billy snorted, "Are you crazy? You do security here in the Keys, what, a couple or three months out of the year, the rest of the time I'm touring. You're not worth fifty percent. You think you're the only one on the payroll?"

"I'm the only one that can throw your ass in jail with a snap of my fingers . . . dude," he said sarcastically.

"Yeah, right, and you would be in the same cell with me if you tried a dumb shit thing like that."

Polk's face twisted into a contemptuous grin, "Billy Boy, how long do you think you would live once I got you into a cell. Prisoners die all the time inside, some by hanging, others by bleeding out from deep arterial cuts. I'm thinking yours would be something deviant like a gang rape, yeah, that would work."

"You sick fuck. You're nothing to me, I'm Billy Fucking Rocket, man. People love me, I'm magic, you could never do anything to hurt me without the world coming down on you. You're a little fish in a little pond, I throw you some chum and you think all of a sudden, you're a big fucking trophy game fish? But really, dude, you run traffic for me from the bight to the Shark. You call that a big deal? Ha! I can pick up the phone and have my man in Tallahassee on your ass in a heartbeat."

Polk swung the streetsweeper hitting Billy's jaw. Billy stumbled back onto a table knocking over a tub of money that scattered across the floor.

"You little turd, you're not calling anyone. Don't tell me your buddies with that goody two shoes, Bill Price, with the Florida agency. Don't you know he's playing pattycakes with Marsh's side-girl, Coco Duvalier. I'd like to do her myself if she wasn't such a stuck-up bitch."

Billy was shaking blood from his damaged mouth. He spat out a piece of tooth, and ran his tongue across the jagged area, astonished that it was only one. His vision was blurred, Polk moved in slow motion. Polk kicked Billy in the shin sending him to the floor.

"Sit there and try to comprehend what I am about to tell you, smartass. We're going box all this cash up and have a couple of your boys load it aboard the *Lucky Lady*. Once we have all '*our*' money and product aboard, we are going to lock up Casa Rocket because we won't be back for a while. We'll pay off the boys and send them on their way. After that you and I and a couple of my guests are going to motor on out of here."

"Where are we going?" It took every ounce of strength to suck up the pain to get the words out.

"Why, we're going to follow the money, '*dude*'. I know it's in George Town somewhere, I just don't know which bank or the account number, but I'm feeling pretty confident that you are going to tell me."

"Never! I'm not telling you anything." Billy got on all fours to get up.

Polk raised the stock of the scatter gun and came down hard on Billy's left hand. The butt breaking bone and cartilage.

Billy shrieked in agony and fell back to the floor cradling his mangled hand. Rods of pain smashed through torn ligaments and fractured knuckles

"What the fuck! . . . what the fuck! Ooooh, you've ruined my hand, oooh, it hurts."

"Of course, it hurts, ya little prick, it's supposed to hurt," he sneered. "The other hand is next . . ."

The counting room door burst open and Fat Man tumbled in falling to the floor. The purple haired freak was right behind him. Polk shot the kid in the chest throwing him back into the hallway. He slid down the far wall leaving a fresco of blood.

Fat Man rolled over with both hands in the air, "Don't shoot, don't shoot . . . I got kids, don't shoot, please."

Polk paused, motioning for Fat Man to get up, "Get over here and start picking up all this money."

Billy sat crying cradling his hand, rocking back and forth. If he could get up, he could make it to the cabinet drawer with the pistol in it.

"Don't even think it, my man. I can read your stupid mind. I've been dealing with punks like you all my life and not a one was ever smart enough to fool me. What are you thinking, you going for a gun stashed here in the room somewhere? Maybe over there in the filing cabinet," he said, as he pulled the top drawer open, slammed opened the second, "Ah ha, *BINGO!* See what I'm saying? A pea shooter, not big enough to kill, but big enough to ruin your day."

Billy pulled himself up with his good hand and stood swaying, "Now what, Polk?"

"I need the name and number of your account in the Cayman. You give it to me, I swear I'll take you with me, leave enough in the account for you to live large the rest of your life. You lie to me and you're a dead man."

"How do I know I can trust you? What's stopping you from taking all the money and killing me?"

"Billy, Billy, would I do that?"

The angelic innocence on Polk's face was meant to reassure Billy, but rather, it had the opposite effect. Billy shook his head no, "I don't trust you. You're a dirty cop, you would kill me to cover your ass in a heartbeat."

Polk made clucking sounds, "Oh Billy, we have a problem then, don't we? I want the numbers and you don't want to give them to me. Let's do this, let's play a little Russian roulette. I'll count to ten, if you don't give me the numbers by the end of the count, I'll shoot Fat Man. You give me the numbers and Fat Man lives another day to go home to his kids. How does that sound?"

"Wha . . . no fucking way!" Fat Man screamed. "*Jeezus*, you fucking guys are crazy. I got kids . . . give him the numbers, Boss, please?"

"Shut up, ya' tub of guts, you don't have any say so in this. This is on Billy." He thumbed back the hammer on the revolver. "Ten . . . Nine . . ."

Billy's pulse redlined. '*Polk was insane. There was no doubt he would kill Terry "Fat Man", but to give him the nums would leave him penniless. All the chances, and risk would have been for nothing. But Fat Man had been a good friend since the early days when he would bust heads when concert goers would get out of hand. He had watched over him like a big brother for years . . .*'

"Six . . . five . . . running out of Fat Man's time on earth, *dude*."

"Stop, Polk, this is insane."

"Four . . . three . . ."

"Billy, tell him for God's sake," Fat Man pleaded. "Don't do this . . ."

"Two . . ."

"Okay! Okay! I'll tell you."

"Talk."

Fat Man had fainted into a pile on the floor.

Billy ripped his shirt off and raised his right arm. A series of numbers had been tattooed into the flesh of the armpit.

"Here's the numbers, you bastard. You better keep your word, or I'll hound you to the ends of the earth."

"Oh, Billy, stop being so dramatic. I said I would leave some for you. Now, let's wake up Fat Man and have him carry all these tubs to the boat."

"I need to do something about my hand, you fuck. My cord hand is destroyed. I need to get to a hospital."

"You won't see a doctor until we hit the Cayman. Do a speedball for the pain, you'll feel fine."

Fat Man bounced back from his near-death experience with a glad heart, quick to jump to at every command from Polk. He loaded three tubs of money on to a push dolly, threw a raincoat from the hall closet over the stack and pulled it out to the dock, followed by Polk holding the street sweeper on his hip and the revolver tucked in his waist band, and Billy hunched forward cupping his destroyed hand.

The prognosticators at NOAA were loving the storm that sat spinning over Cuba, the Keys, and South Florida. It wasn't gaining or losing strength nor moving, it just sat and spun like a crazed dervish, throwing out spears of lightning and powder kegs of thunder. The boys in the know thought it might just beat itself out in a few days but a high across the Midwest colliding with a low from the east might push it south. Didn't make sense to anyone, but that's what was being reported twenty-four hours a day.

Fat Man weighed three ten in his birthday suit and wasn't very well coordinated. So, when he took a nose dive over the swim step boarding the *Lucky Lady* no one was surprised, except perhaps himself. The tub of money hit the deck on its side and bundles of hundred scattered across the wet deck.

"Ya' dumb donkey, get that money picked up before any flows out the scuppers," Polk yelled over the wind.

The boat's deck lights came on, momentarily stealing Polk's night vision.

Billy's muscle man, Marcus, was standing on the fly bridge in a yellow slicker, "What the hell's going on down there? Billy? Is that you? Polk? What the hell?"

"Get down here and help Fat Man get these tubs aboard," Polk yelled.

"Do as he says, Marky. I'm hurt and need to get aboard, and have you look at my hand."

Marcus hustled down the ladder and did as Billy had ordered.

"Damn, I'm glad you're here. That frigging cab driver, Maxi, is driving me crazy. He hasn't stop talking since he came aboard with the kid."

"What kid?" Polk demanded sharply.

"Sheila's kid, Mikey. He hasn't stopped crying either, since he came aboard. I gave him ice cream, but he just keeps blubbering for his mother. I was thinking about knocking him in a sack and throwing him overboard. I finally locked him up in one of the crew cabins."

"So, this is where the little shit has been hiding?"

"Pardon?" Marcus asked, trying to hear over the howling wind.

"Nothing. Get this money picked up."

Mikey was a loose end; the little shit was the only person that could finger him in the killing of Sheila Pollack. The bitch earned it. No chick is ever going to turn him down, especially a whore like Sheila. Killing her was especially enjoyable because she was tied to Jack

Marsh and that bitch that passes herself off as a granddaughter to Haiti's notorious President, Baby Doc Duvalier, Coco.

Chapter 19

The air in the crew cabin stunk. Little Mikey had soiled himself earlier when he was brought aboard, fearful of the scary man that hurt his arm as he yanked him about. The small room became even more fetid when Max and Renée were pushed inside, and the door locked behind them. Renée had peed herself sometime during her blackout state. Max was afraid to move out of fear that he would do number one and two if he didn't get to a head soon.

"This sucks, Mikey. We're being treated as prisoners instead of employees. When Billy comes aboard I'll get this straightened out, PDQ, believe me."

"Whath's PDQ mean, Mithster Max?" He asked, lisping in his child's tongue.

"It don't mean nothing in the regular world, son. In my world, it means I'm going to kick some serious ass when I get my hands on the big palooka what has us locked in here."

"I know what ass is, my momma says that word all the time. She call's some of her boyfriend's stupid ass."

"Hey, watch your mouth kid or I'll smack ya," Max said.

The *Lucky Lady* was a luxurious seventy-three-foot ocean going yacht befitting a rock star like Billy Rocket. The main deck was lavishly appointed in dark teak decks, polished brass fixtures, tropical floral and sea life island themed cut-glass splendor in all the beautiful vibrant colors of the sea. The well tricked out stainless steel galley appointed with state of the art equipment was off a spacious glass topped dining area frosted with coral and teal colors, with a head forward of a large plush vanilla salon tossed about with large comfortable duck down toss pillows of the same color theme. The three large crew quarters were below decks forward of the engine room. The engine room was something of an art to behold. It was a canvas of polished chrome everywhere the eye danced and crowded with two Cat C-30's that delivered fifteen hundred horse power when called on. The refrigeration unit, water purifier, generator, batteries and fixtures were crammed in the space. It was, also, where Billy stashed the incoming kilos of cocaine, ecstasy pills, weed from the Cayman and tubs of money heading back down to the islands. The whole arrangement gave drug running a splendiferous appearance suitable for a man of Billy's notoriety. The Rocket Man may be past his prime and generation of music, but his fans and groupies still loved his shit, and he just kept on providing it, as he sang and pranced around a stage like he did twenty years before when he was a young man.

"Shhh. What was that?" Max put his ear to the hatch door. "Sounds like something landed on the deck."

"Wha . . . where am I?" Renée slurred. "Oh, my God, what did I take? I feel like my head is about to explode."

A corner of the sheet she was swathed in fell away exposing a breast. Max and Mikey looked at it for a moment, both for different reasons, then Mikey pulled the sheet up to cover it.

"Renée, it's me Max Simms. Remember, I'm Jack Marsh's best friend. I saved you from tragedy that you wouldn't believe, and now we're in danger."

"Max Simms? Oh, my God! I didn't do you, did I?"

Max's eyes flashed in anger, "If you did, you would remember it, sugar."

"Max, I hear the monster man. It's him, he's coming for me." Mikey said, terror in his eyes.

"What are you saying, Mikey. What monster man? You mean Marcus, the mutt that locked us in here?"

"No . . . no, the man that hurt my momma."

"That's Sheriff Polk, I would know that voice anywhere, He's a rotten bastard," Renée whispered

Max put his ear to the door and a finger to his mouth, "Shhhh."

Polk's voice boomed loud in the main cabin.

"Get these tubs stowed below, I want to be underway in the next fifteen minutes."

Above, Marcus shot a look over to his boss, Billy, for confirmation.

"Don't bother asking him, I'm the new rock star around here, you'll be taking orders from me until I say otherwise. Set a course for George Town. When we pull out of here, I want this bucket at full throttle."

"What should I do, Billy . . .?"

"I told you what you should do. I'm in charge now," Polk screamed. "You don't want to fuck with me, Marcus, not tonight, not ever."

"I said, do as he says," Billy mumbled.

The cabin door slid open and a guy backed in pulling a limp body by the hands.

"I don't like this, Billy. Steve was my friend and now look at him, he's dead. That cocksucker killed him. What's happening to us Billy? I'm scared."

"Shut up and go get the punk in the hallway. Fat Man, get your ass out to the patrol car and get the old broad aboard. We've got ten minutes and then it's sayonara, Key West," Polk commanded. "And, don't forget the naked guy on the floorboard."

For an instant, the room froze in time, Polk was outnumbered. It wouldn't take much to overwhelm him, even with a pistol in his hand, they could do it, Billy thought, then it passed. They were fucked.

"Like I said before, do as he says!"

The *Lucky Lady* eased away from the dock, her props turning just enough to move her through the darkness on a 270° course. Without her running lights on, she was invisible, blending in with the mangroves on either side of the channel. The dredged channel was narrow, one small twitch and she would career off the coral walls.

The electronics on the bridge threw off a soft green glow that gave everyone on the crowded bridge a deathly pallor. The pounding rain and vibration from the twin diesel engines would have been soothing if it weren't for Polk brandishing the shotgun.

"I'm going to lose my bowels, Billy," Fat Man said. "I gotta go right now, Sheriff, swear to God."

"Ya' tub of guts, don't do it up here, it's bad enough that I have to look at ya'. I don't want to be smelling you for the next couple of days."

"I have to peepee, Sheriff, can I go, too?" The kid, Mikey asked, with his friend's blood all over his hands and arms asked.

"Jesus, what is this, preschool? Both of ya' get below and do your business then get back up here . . . and wash that blood off."

"Come on, dude, but I get to go first," Fat Man said to the child.

"Hurry back, I'll go next," Billy said.

Both men hurried down the steps into the main deck parlor. Terry grabbed the guy's arms and pulled him in close.

"Shhh. Don't say anything. We're going over the side," he whispered.

"But what about Billy?"

"Billy's smarter than Polk any day, he'll figure out something, but this is our only chance. That fucker will kill us as soon as he can, we've seen too much."

"But what if he kills Billy, and what about the old lady, she's hurt bad."

"Well, stay if you want, but I'm out of here," Fat Man said, and slid the aft hatch open leading to the back deck.

The new guy was right behind him. They swung over the transom onto the dive platform and jumped. The night and the rain quickly swallowed them up. Fat Man was a poor swimmer, but could dog paddle like an Olympian despite his weight bobbing him up and down like a fishing cork.

"Hey, wait up for me," he yelled.

Behind him, the *Lucky Lady* had disappeared into the night.

Chapter 20

Jack was fighting to stay conscious. He was exhausted. The bullet from the chopper had dug a shallow furrow along the left side of his head that still seeped blood. His jaw hurt like hell, and his tongue was raw from rubbing against the jagged tooth. Every muscle in his body ached, and he was starving. He couldn't remember the last time he had anything to eat. He would never turn his nose up again to Cookie's collards and cornbread, well, maybe not the cornbread. He brought the Grady White boat off plane and let her settle into the roiling bay waters.

He turned the cuddy cabin light on and was surprised that Luther had propped himself up on the bench. Both men stared at each other for a moment."

"What?" Jack said.

"I been thinking, Mister Jack. It appears to me that we have a problem."

"What the hell are you talking about, What problem?"

"Oh yes, we have a problem. You and me. That old color problem."

"Jesus, Luther, this is no time to be talking bullshit."

Jack was rummaging through storage lockers, found a can of sausages and ripped the top off.

"I contacted the *Queen*. We'll hook up with her in another hour then we are safe." He extended the can to share the tasteless wieners.

"That's what I'm talking about, Jack. We hook up with your people and then what? We go back to Key West, or wherever, and the law comes poking around and you turn over the black dude to save your white ass."

Jack pulled the can back in thought, staring into the black eyes. Lightning cracked so close both men flinched.

"Luther. I'll tell you this one time, and that's all. The minute you cut me down and untied my hands, you became more to me than a brother. We are joined forever. When a man saves another man's life, he owes a debt that can never be repaid. I don't care anything about your color, or your uppity parents and your bullshit car, or your white girlfriend. You and I will always be a part of each other."

Luther was quiet, pain written across his face, "I must be delirious, I believe some of that bullshit you just said, Marsh. For now, I just want to live long enough to see how this turns out. There'll be time enough for pretty talk, later."

Jack found a quart of Hennessy brandy and broke the seal. He stared at it for a long moment, his whole being screaming for it, he hungered for it, he needed it. His hand shook, he raised it to his mouth . . .

Luther snatched it from his hand, "That makes twice I've saved your ass, Jack. You'll owe me . . . forever."

Jack's hands shook, the acidic taste of burning adrenaline made him sick. He hurried up on deck and vomited over the side. The wind blew bile back on to his bare chest, a cold shiver shook him. He had the urge to jump overboard and swim until he sank. He was filled with disgust and loathing at his weakness. He was weary of the constant worry for others, the responsibility for so many that depended on him, always trying to take care of others, making sure that they were safe, it was too much.

He stood, stripping off the trousers he had taken from the prison hut, trousers that belonged to a dead man. Letting the rain pour over him, washing off the stench from the camp and the putrid water of the everglades. He scrubbed himself with his hands, running his fingers through his hair, across his face and chest. His groin was swollen and tender to the touch where he had been kicked and then invaded by a horde of primordial nameless biting and stinging pests.

The more he scrubbed the better he felt. Each splash of rain was like a metaphysical healing. His mind cleared, and the tiredness melted away. The pain was still there to be sure, but under control. The rain filled his mouth and cleansed his nose and eyes of grunge. He quenched his thirst and cleared his nose, he was beginning to feel alive, again.

He pulled on swim trunks and a rash guard he found in a stowage locker below. The rash guard was tight but felt good against his sore muscles.

"Thank God, you finally covered that up, Jack, I was beginning to feel sorry for the little guy," Luther said.

"Stow it, Luther, that little guy is a legend in his own time."

"Yeah, right, and I'm Bill Gates."

He rummaged through a food locker and came up with a box of raisins and tossed a handful into his mouth, chewed quickly and swallowed. A can of sardines followed the raisins. He held the raisin box out to Luther to take.

"No thanks, I'm sticking with the brandy."

The going was slow, waves were breaking huge over the bow in one instant and slamming it down in a trough the next. Jack kept the craft pointed south, riding the turbulent storm. The waters in Florida Bay were shallow, no more than ten to twelve feet in some areas that quickly rose to two to three feet. In the best of weather, the Bay was dangerous if you didn't know what you were doing and even if you thought you knew it, it would jump up and rip you open from stem to stern. The depth gage couldn't keep up with the rapid rise and fall of the hull

Garbled voices of distress crackled over channel 16. Jack tried to make since of the exchange but gave up. It seemed that two or three different people were on the line all speaking at once. Only crazy people would be out on the water in this storm, what did they expect, even the US Coast Guard wasn't out unless it was a matter of life or death.

Jack tried to reach Bull on the radio with no luck, they had agreed that Bull should wait for him off the west entrance of Bahia Honda channel. Bull was to run out storm anchors and wait. The *Queen* would tear her bottom out if he tried to hook up with Jack anywhere north of Marathon, one small degree off and she would be gutted.

A brightening of the storm clouds to the east was the only sign that dawn was breaking. *NOAA* was cycling the same weather report over and over. Jack tuned it out and held the wheel tight. The prison camp was well behind them, but fear of capture tugged at the hair on his neck. He was resolved that he would not go back if they discovered them out here on the water, he would rather die on his terms than those psycho bastards running that death camp. How could that place exist in America? Even the discomfort of waterboarding paled in comparison to the madness he had experienced. Watching the men shuffling by barefooted with insect swollen legs into thatch huts reminded him of the films of allied troops imprisoned and starved in Burma and

Malaysia in World War Two. If he made it out of this fix alive, he was going to blow this wide open, starting with Polk and that sadistic Major Cotton, even the governor if he was involved. Was Bill Price, Coco's boyfriend and sometime lover with the Florida Bureau of Investigation involved somehow? How deep was the corruption?

Jack's thoughts were on vengeance, the people in charge of the law were worse than the lawbreakers. It's a clear case of the patients running the asylum., the problem was, he didn't know how deep the insanity ran, who were the masterminds and who were the gatekeepers. Were all the Monroe County deputies Polk's marionettes, played for his purposes. Jack thought back on the shakedown Polk and Deputy Kilpatrick tried to pull on him years ago and then the night Kilpatrick was killed in the warehouse bust. Polk was dirty then and he is dirty now and swimming in a much bigger pond. He knew he wouldn't make it ashore alive if Polk was in the search team, for sure he had given orders to shoot to kill.

Chapter 21

At 0930 Jack was back in touch with Bull on the *Queen* by radio. Twenty minutes later he pulled up alongside the portside of the *Queen* and threw a line up to Lamont's eager hands and grinning face.

"I told 'em they couldn't hold you down, Mister Jack. I said you was one crazy white dude, and the jail ain't been built that can hold you."

"Jump down here and give me a hand. I have a wounded man aboard."

The deck was lined with Coco, Jinx, Scarlet, and Cookie all smiling. Bull was on the bridge watching, his forehead wrinkled with worry. They exchanged looks understanding trouble rode the wind.

"Lord, what happened to this man? Is he dead?" Lamont asked, pulling a blood-soaked towel from Luther's body. "Smells like he drank himself to death, too, must have been some good shit, Jack."

"I'm not dead yet. Another ten minutes of pounding waves and I would be though," Luther groaned.

"It's alive, Jack. It talks." Lamont faked surprise. "If it had blood, it would look like a brother."

"Lamont, lets' do the *'Brother'* routine later. Let's get him over to the *Queen*."

"Amen to that Jack. Bull says all hell's breaking loose up on the mainland. He says that twenty-something prisoners burned to death out in a work camp. Another dozen been shot in a riot. Supposed to be five or six guard's dead or missing. The state troopers and county sheriff's deputies have Highway 1 locked down tighter than a school girl's tush. They are talking about sending down some National Guard boys from Miami."

Lamont's words were spoken fast and clipped as they lugged Luther over the gunwale. Jinx and Coco grabbed out helping hands. The move to the main cabin was clumsy and painful, Cookie ran ahead and had the first aid kit out by the time they had him inside.

"Trow' him up here on the table, Jack, let me take a look at him," Cookie said.

Cookie mumbled as his boney fingers probed the wound.

"Mmm hmm, yep, uh-huh, oh Lordy . . ."

"What?" Jack asked alarmed.

"Dis' man been shot."

Coco rolled her eyes, and stepped in elbowing Cookie out of the way. "Let me take care of this."

Her hands plucked at the seeping wound pulling bits of twigs, dirt, sand, and infected scabs away. Luther grunted in pain when she probed the jagged wound with a finger.

"Boil water, Cookie," she commanded. "Jinx, grab the halogen lamp from the bridge, you'll need to hold it for me. Scarlet, bring towels from below, we'll need them."

She took scissors from the kit and cut away the filthy shorts from Luther's body, and dropped them to the deck. As she waited for her helpers to bring what she needed she examined the semiconscious man before her. She gasped when she studied his broad back, muscled from hard work, it was covered with dozens of crisscrossing slashes and deep cuts, some were fresh, others scarred over. His shoulders and neck were thick and strong. She turned his head to study his face and saw how handsome he was, even with the insect swollen eyes and the cracked lips, she was taken with his beauty. Something deep inside of her sparked and spread. She wanted to bend forward and kiss him, and whisper for him not to worry or die, she would take care of him. The flicker stayed with her as she brought her attention back to the wound.

"Let's hurry, this man needs us to move fast." She busied herself cleaning the wound.

Bull bounced down from the bridge, the worry lines furrowed deep.

"Jack, what the hell did they do to you guys?" Bull asked.

Jack stepped back from the mess table swooning. The hours of standing at the helm of the small craft had left him exhausted. His equilibrium was off from the constant rocking and beating of the storm. In comparison, the *Queen* was like standing in the Searstown parking lot. He collapsed back into one of the chairs.

"Long story, Bull. Update me on what's happening."

"Jeez, Jack, there's a shit storm all over South Florida. Whatever happened at that work camp has made international news. Every law agency in the country has boots on the ground in and around Florida City. Highway 1 is closed to all traffic, holding up southbound traffic all the way back to 836 and Miami International," he said looking closely into Jack's eyes. "That ain't all. Warden Cotton is saying you were the ring leader of the riot, says that you killed three of his deputies and a couple of trustees before they killed you. He said that his lead team of experts found your chard body among the work camp with a gun in your hand."

Jack's laugh hurt, "Cotton always was a dumb ass. He's always thought the bigger the lie the more believable it will be. The only charred bodies he'll find are of his own making. If he thinks I'm dead, that's good for now, but he's going to pay for what he did to me."

"That's not all Jack, we've got big trouble right here of our own. Judge Powers is MIA and we think Polk has her. She went to his place to find out why he had you moved from Key West up to Florida City without a bench warrant or something. She was supposed to see him and then scoot back here to the *Queen*, that was last night, and we haven't heard anything from her since."

Jack nodded over to Jinx and raised his eyebrows in question.

Bull whispered, "He's okay, worried sick, but he's tough. Down deep inside he loves the old broad but he's keeping it under wraps."

Scarlet sat on the arm of the chair and began cleaning Jack's face and scalp wound, daubing cautiously as he winced with each touch.

"Mister Marsh, I want you to know how sorry I am for not being straight up with you and Miss Coco. We didn't mean anything like this to happen, honest," she began to cry again.

"What's she saying, Bull?"

"Judge Madge is just part of the problem. It seems that Scarlet, Sheila, and Renée have been doing some heavy partying with Billy Rocket and his groupies out on Shark Key lately . . ."

"I don't have a clue of what you're talking about, Chief. Who the hell is Billy Rocket?" Jack said.

Bull laid it all out for him as briefly as possible about the drugs and wild parties.

"Sheila's murderer is probably one of the groupies or even Billy himself or, get this, Sheriff Polk.

"Polk!" Jack exclaimed.

"Yeah, Polk. It gets crazier. Polk was there for a lot of the parties and even had a thing for Sheila, but according to Scarlet here, she couldn't stand him, refused to sleep with him, and he would spin out of control and threaten her."

"I hope what I'm thinking isn't correct, but it's beginning to make sense to me, Chief. Is it possible that Polk raped and killed Sheila because of her rejection then pinned it on me because I knew about him killing Kilpatrick? I know it sounds insane, but it could be possible."

"More than possible. Hear me out, it gets worse. Max found Sheila's boy, Mikey, but refused to bring him to the Sand Bar, because the kid said his mom's killer had blue eyes. So dumb ass Max puts two and two together and comes up with three. He says that Mathew Turner kid we called Blue has blue eyes, so he must be the killer and refuses to bring him over. He says he was going to take Mikey someplace where he would be much safer . . . Billy Rocket's"

Jack looked around, "Where is Blue?"

"In the wind. Lamont dropped him off at the halfway house, but the house mouse said he never showed. Coco found a letter penciled to you and him saying he was skipping out. He says he didn't kill Sheila, but no one would believe him because he was a con and there was no way he would ever go back to prison again. He said thanks for all your help and, *poof,* gone."

"*AGHHHH!*" Luther screamed out.

"Hold him tight, Cookie. I'll be out of here in a few seconds," Coco said, as she dug deep into Luther's wound with a thin filet knife. She worked it back and forth, backing the blade out centimeter by centimeter.

Jack and Bull watched from their seats in awe at the macabre site, as a beautiful woman of Haitian and French European heritage with her hair flowing in lengthy ringlets tied up in an African headscarf, bent over a black man whose white round eyes and strong teeth were locked in pain as she dug a knife into his back. Adding to the moment, was the white man in a tweed jacket with leather elbows holding a light over the scene looking morbidly on, and a tall skinny black man with heels digging in pulling on Luther's arms.

"Got it," Coco said, proudly holding up a slug between bloody fingers. "I have no idea what I'm saying, but I think it missed the kidney and just damaged muscle. If he starts peeing blood, he can sue me, but for now, at least he's alive."

"Cookie, bring up a bunk mattress from the crew's birth. We'll keep him up here, so we can watch him," Chief Bull ordered.

"Yes, sir, Cap'n"

"It gets even worse, Jack," Bull was back on topic. "Seems like there has been a lot of action out on Shark Key, too. The county boys are all over the Key. Some Rent-A-Cop at the front gate is yapping his head off. He says that around midnight, Sheriff Polk plowed into a southbound vehicle, killing the driver. Polk was thrown clear of the accident into a ditch. The two deputies on permanent duty across from the gate began traffic control as Polk left the scene driving one of the patrol cars. And get this, Polk was driving *my* truck!"

Jack sat listening, trying to make sense of it all. How was it even possible for all this to have happened in four days, or was it three, he couldn't remember.

"Everything points to Shark Key, Bull. Let's get over there and get our people back."

"Just one thing, Jack. Shark Key has been a called a crime scene and no one is getting on or off the Key. A couple of Billy Boy's bodyguards were busted along with a few groupies stoned out of their minds. One of the women had to be choppered up to Miami Medical in a straightjacket, according to the scanner talk she had a split tongue and was yelling something about Billy being god and she was his goddess."

"What about our people?"

"One of the bodyguards said that Polk had a gun on him and Billy and made them load tubs of cash from one of the rooms onto a dolly then take them out to Billy's yacht waiting at the dock. Once aboard, Polk made him, and his friend carry three bodies aboard. He told the cops that he didn't want any part of what was going on, so he and his friend jumped in the canal and swam away, hiding in the mangroves until the yacht had disappeared into the storm."

"So, old Polk is on a boat somewhere out here in this storm? Let's go get him, Chief. I want him, and I want him bad."

"They have like a seven-hour lead on us, Jack." He looked at his watch, "Eight hours."

"What about Mikey and Max, any word on them?"

"They're aboard too, and so is Renée and Jack, . . . so is Judge Powers."

Jack looked down to Scarlet who had sat on the floor listening to Bull lay everything out.

"Any idea where they might be going, Scarlet. Any clue that would help us."

"I heard Marcus and Bones talking about someplace called George Town a few times and the fun they had visiting there, but I don't think they were the college type, know what I mean. Those two guys were bozos from nowhere. I'll bet they never finished high school."

Jack's left eye flickered as it often did when he thought he was being played.

"You thinking what I'm thinking, Jack?"

"I do believe so. Are we provisioned up?"

"Yep, topped off and ship shape."

"Then let's kick her in the ass and run them down."

"Mister Marsh, if you're saying you're going to chase down Billy's boat, I don't know if you can. Billy let me steer it once when we went out to the Tortugas for a snorkeling party. It is really fast, Marcus got mad at Billy when he saw me driving the boat. That was the only time I ever heard Marcus argue with Billy. He said at that speed, one crazy twist of the wheel and there would be trouble."

Bull rolled his eyes, not putting much credence into Scarlet's testimony of danger. The *Queen* could run down just about any civilian ship in the Caribbean Sea. No production boat was afloat that he couldn't hunt down, he was ticketed for Master, any vessel, any ocean.

"Jack, just give the order and I'll run an intersecting course. The *Queen's* ready," he said proudly.

"What about Luther? Can he travel, or do we need to drop him off in Marathon? Fisherman's Hospital is right across from the Yacht Club, we could walk him across and be back aboard in twenty minutes."

"Hey, you're not getting rid of me like that. These Rednecks see a Brother and they'll call the law in heartbeat, swearing I stole something. I'm going with you, Jack."

Jack grinned and winked, "Yas, suh, we's gots to be in Cairo by morning time. They's after us." Jack quoted from Huck Finn's words.

Bull laughed at the exchange as the others looked on bewildered.

"By the way, Scarlet, What's the name of Billy's boat."

"Well, unless he's changed it, that is, since I was on it, its named *Lucky Lady*. He said he named it for me because I was about to become the luckiest lady in the world, but I didn't believe him since that was my first time being on it, you know what I'm saying?"

Jack's eye twitched, and the thought was gone.

Chapter 22

The *Lady* plowed through the storm on a southerly course, taking the roiling seas with her stabilizers acting as giant pectoral fins. Even so, the sea is always the master with little respect for man and lifted and slammed her at will. A weak light separated the day from the night revealing heavy storm torn clouds twirling and ripping across the sky throwing sheets of rain as they went. On the bridge, the scene matched the seas, Polk stood next to Marcus at the helm brandishing his pistol shouting in anger.

"Those chickenshits jumped ship and you knew it," Polk screamed insanely. "You better hope that they drown, or your ugly ass will be joining them."

"I didn't know they were going to split. They said they had to take a leak, so what's not to believe. Don't sweat it, Terry doesn't know how to swim, and Bob is scared of his own shadow? Even if they make it back to the dock they'll be gone, probably won't slow down until they hit Disney World."

Polk was exhausted, the last twelve hours had been beyond stressful. He never intended for things in the Keys to end this way. He had always pictured himself retiring as Sheriff of Monroe County and then fade away to the Islands, with a brief stop off to visit his money in Grand Cayman. On his last visit to the *'Neverlands'*, as he called the Bank of Netherlands in George Town, he had added another seven hundred thousand to his war chest of four million. Now, with Billy's tubs of cash, he would be set for five life times. Hell, he might even buy a place in Rio, lots of pretty girls and boys down there.

"Billy, bring the kid up here, I need to have a talk with him."

"Fuck you, Polk. You want the kid, you get him yourself," Billy said around the ice pack he was holding to his swollen and broken mouth and damaged hand.

"Get the kid, Marcus, I need to have a come to Jesus minute with your boss here."

"Whatever you say, Sheriff. I have the helm locked on 200° but you need to stand by in case she slips out of auto. She's a quick-triggered bitch."

Polk took the captain's chair and swiveled around so he could see Billy stretched out on the cushioned bench that ran around the portside of the bridge

"Billy, you need to work with me here. You know we are both in this together, the cops are all over your place and anyone still there is singing like a Keys Chicken. By now, they know all about your drug and laundering business, and my protecting you, not to mention the broads we partied hard with. We can never go back, we need to work this out between us, there's enough money for us to live large forever, if we can work together. You'll have to lay off the white shit though. I can't allow that. Cervezas are one thing but the powder has got to cease and desist."

"Polk, the only reason I'm even talking to you is because of the gun in your hand. You're nothing to me, you were such a small piece of my world that you didn't even register on my radar except when I needed help on the deliveries and drop offs every few months." The more Billy talked, the more pissed he became. "You're a stone-cold killer, Polk. You killed Stevie right in front of Terry and me not more than a few hours ago, there's a body below decks that you brought with you and an old woman that is probably going to die any minute now, if she hasn't already, and you want me to partner up with you? Are you fucking crazy?"

Polk's eyes flashed then went dead. "You punk, you think I'm crazy? Do you? *DO YOU?*" he screamed. "You know what it's like growing up in the real Florida, moving from one camp to the next picking oranges one place, limes at another, melons, more oranges for a dollar a bucket when you're a kid. There wasn't any sunny sand beaches or pretty girls to play with for me. For me, there was just a beating from an alcoholic old man if I didn't keep up with the other kids picking. Fuck you and your glittery costumes and your stupid music. Try wearing the same clothes for months at a time, the only bath was in one of the canals. Yeah, I had long hair like yours, but mine was filled with lice and bugs it wasn't pretty like yours." Polk held a hand up, turning the palm slowly. "Look at these hands, Billy. You ever pick fruit? You ever cry yourself to sleep at night from hundreds of little thorn pricks? Or wasp stings that swell your eyes shut and all the while your old man ragging on your ass in a drunken stupor about what a worthless piece of shit you are? Hold out your hand."

"What?"

"Hold out your good hand."

"Wha . . . why?"

"Hold out your hand, Billy."

"No!"

Polk bounced off the chair, pulled Billy's balled hand clear of his body and shot. The hand exploded in a bloody mist, splinters of bone peppered Billy's face. Shockwaves from the closeness of the shot reverberated through both men. Billy's body spasmed in shock, it threw him from the cushioned bench to the floor jerking insanely.

"What the hell have you done?" Marcus bounded up the steps to the bridge.

"Mind your own business, Marcus. This is between me and Billy. It's on him, not me. I made him an offer that would bring all this craziness to an end. He turned it down, so now it's me alone to see this through."

"I don't know what the hell your talking about, Polk. I only know that you bring trouble with you wherever you go."

Polk ignored him and continued to stare at Billy's unconscious body. He forced himself to take deep breaths, Marcus was right, he needed to slow it down.

"Take the wheel, I'm going out on the deck for a minute," he slid the bridge wing hatch open, and stopped, "And Marcus, don't even try to contact anyone. If you do, everyone on this tub is going down."

Marcus lifted Billy from the deck and grimaced at the mangled hand. Billy was screwed, his guitar days were over. All their days were going to be over if they didn't stop Polk, the guy had totally flipped out. Everyone in the band and the groupies that followed them around the country avoided him whenever he was around, especially the chicks, they didn't want to have anything to do with him. The only time he scored was if the chick was blown out of her gourd. The girls said that he would make them do weird things to him to hurt him.

"Billy, wake up Billy," he whispered. "We need to talk while Polk is out on deck."

Billy didn't respond, his face was drained of blood looking more dead than alive. Marcus jumped back down to the main cabin and pulled the first aid kit free of its bracket and hurried back to the bridge.

"Hold on, Billy, this is going to sting like crazy." He poured iodine over the mangled hand, spilling most of it on the deck. Billy's hand twitched a couple of times then relaxed. Marcus knew that his boss and friend needed help soon or he may lose the function in his hands. On closer inspection, three of the fingers and the thumb were gone.

"Leave him be, and get the kid and Simms up here," Polk ordered from the hatchway. "After you do that toss the two stiffs overboard, the judge too if she's dead."

"Judge? That old lady is a judge? What the fuck! Do you know killing a judge is worse than killing a cop, it's a straight ride on the needle, dude."

"Let me worry about that. No one will ever know what happened to her, she'll just disappear like so many other people when they're old and senile."

Polk took up station again at the helm and busied himself fidgeting with the radio, listening for any updates on the carnage he created at his house and on Shark Key.

There was no going back now, Samuel, no siree. The idea that he was criminal now gave him a visceral thrill.

Max heard the door rattle and gathered his two charges in his boney arms, determined to talk his way out of the situation. His cunning and shrewd use of the language had always served him well. In Rikers, he had the bad boys eating out of his hands once they saw that he was supportive of their cause, no matter what it was as long as it wasn't him. He became known as *'The Fixer'* among the different gangs and grudge fights because of his ability to paint both sides of an argument by the simple ruse of selling both sides out and making them feel good about it.

The door swung open just as a wave tipped the boat to starboard throwing Marcus into the cabin landing on the three shrieking prisoners. Little Mikey was wrapped around Max's neck screeching like a spider monkey, Max pulled Renée across his body for protection. once he realized that it was just the big palooka that locked them in the cabin, he let her go.

"Marcus, you son of a bitch!" Renée screamed. "Why am I locked up in here with this idiot? Get me out of here before he wets himself again."

Marcus held a finger to his mouth to silence them. "We got trouble topside. Billy's hurt bad, one of his hands has been shot real bad, the other is totally broken. He's unconscious on the bridge."

"What about the crew, the others? Where are we going?" Renée was totally confused, her mind still chasing the drug vapors out.

"It's a pig fuck, everything is ruined. The cops are swarming the mansion, Polk has been shooting anyone that doesn't obey his orders, and I'm the only crew member left. The cabin across the passageway has two dead people in it and an old lady that Polk calls the Judge . . ."

"The Judge?" Max said in shock. "Judge Powers? You have to be wrong, what would she be doing with that mutt Polk. She hates him, they fight like a couple of winos over a drink."

"She's not with him, she's his prisoner. She's hurt bad, if we don't get her help soon I think she might die."

"Where is that punk? Let me at him." Max tried to push by Marcus big frame, but not too hard.

"Slow it down, Simms, he wants me to bring you and the kid up to the bridge. I don't like it, he's got this wild look in his eyes. I think he might have hit up with a speedball out on deck."

"You're not leaving me down here in this cabin, Marcus I'm going, too."

"Wrap that sheet around you, honey, I'll protect you and the kid. Nobody's going to fuck with us."

"Where is that punk? Let me at him." Max tried to push by Marcus big frame, but not too hard.

"Slow it down, Simms, he wants me to bring you and the kid up to the bridge. I don't like it, he's got this wild look in his eyes. I think he might have hit a speedball out on deck, he came back in really fucked up."

"You're not leaving me down here in this cabin alone, Marcus, I'm going too," Scarlet jumped up quickly.

"Wrap that sheet around you, honey, I'll protect you and the kid. Nobody's going to mess with us as long as I have a breath in my body," Max said, stepping around Marcus as he was trying to sort himself out.

"Hold on, Simms, we need to talk," Marcus said, pulling free from the tangled bodies. "Polk is off his rocker, he's totally flipped out. He has us on a course for George Town in the Cayman. I know he's going to get rid of all of us once we get there, he won't have any need for us once Billy's money is tucked away."

Max's ears pricked up at the mention of money. "What kind of money we talking about here, Marcus?"

"Tubs of it, it's Billy's take from the drug sales from the last tour we were on. Probably a load of dime bags mixed in with it. I didn't go through it, Max, I've been kind of busy here."

"Where did ya put the tubs?"

"Why, you thinking about bailing out on me like Terry and Bob did, fuckers jumped ship before we were clear of the dock."

"Nah, just curious, it's my nature to know all the facts," he said, as he stroked his chin in thought. He snapped his fingers, and said, "I got it, we'll act like we're on his side, maybe give up Renée to show that we're sincere . . ."

"MAX!!!!" Renée screamed. "Marcus, kill this creature right now before he gets us all killed."

"Not too cool, Simms. We're going to need a better plan than that. If he sees we're playing him, he'll kill us for sure. I say we just go along with what he says and keep our eyes open for some kind of opportunity. He has to sleep sometime, maybe we can jump him then."

"I want my momma," Mikey wailed.

Renée pulled Mikey to her bosom, "It's okay, little man, everything is going to be just fine. You just stay close to me and do as I say," she flashed her eyes over to Max, "and don't listen to what Mister Simms says and you'll be just fine."

Max made a *pffft* sound through his rabbit teeth as Mikey burrowed into her bosom sniffling. "Whatever."

"Marcus, get the kid up here, now," Polk yelled, over the boat's sound system.

"We're on our way," Marcus bellowed back.

The group clung together as they made their way topside to the bridge, looking like refugees about to meet their fate.

"What a pathetic bunch of idiots. You'd think I was some kind of monster. Get up here and let me take a look at you," he said, brandishing the pistol.

Max pushed away from the group, "Listen, Sheriff, I know we've had our differences in the past, but I never held a grudge. The way I see it is that we're in deep trouble here and we need to work together to get out of this mess. I want to offer my services as a good citizen of Key West to help you in any way that I can. You just say the word and I'm with you."

Marcus and Renée looked on astonished at the capitulation of one of their allies of only a few moments ago.

Polk looked him up and down suspiciously. He knew Simms was a weasel and would sell his soul for a half a buck, but this may work in his favor.

"Thanks, Max, I could use some loyalty for a change. We've got a long next couple of days and I'll need someone to watch my back."

"I'm your man, Sheriff. Times like this, fellow students of the law need to stick together."

"Okay, I like that, Max. Come over here and take the helm."

"Aye Aye, Skipper, I've got the helm," Max snapped out.

"Keep an ear on the radio too, all hell is breaking loose up on the mainland."

Polk stood with his hands on his hips sneering at the others,

"Hello, Renée. That burn healing okay?"

"Screw you, Polk. I told Billy what you did to me and he said he would take care of you."

"Poor Billy's not taking care of anyone, Puss. He's a little busy taking care of himself right now."

Renée noticed Billy on the deck for the first time and ran to him. "Billy, my God, look at your face, what happened . . ." Then she spotted his hands and fainted.

Mikey ran to her side crying. Polk jerked him up by one hand and carried him hanging a few inches off the deck to the helm. He snapped a cuff onto a tiny wrist and the other to the wheel.

"You're not disappearing from me again, you little shit. You've caused me enough grief as it is," he growled.

He turned his attention to Marcus, "Come with me, we'll dump the two stiffs overboard."

"What about the old woman?"

"What about her? It's not going to matter if she's dead or alive. I'll hang onto her in case I need a bargaining chip. The bitch has friends in high places. She might come in handy."

The crew deck was oddly quiet of the storm noises three decks up. Recessed lights dimly lit the companionway giving the impression of a last mile on death row. Closed cabin doors and gear lockers led the way to the last cabin on the port side. The smell hit both men at the same time, the sickly-sweet stink of a relaxed sphincter.

"Hello, death, my old friend," Polk sang softly, as he pushed the cabin door open.

"How's this for a crime scene, Watson?" Polk said, seemingly off somewhere else. "Why, poor Armand, there you are. Alas, I knew you well, my young and oh so handsome friend."

Polk pulled at Armand's body that was beginning the first stages of rigor.

"Grab his arms, let's do this."

Topside, the sky was churning with heavy clouds scudding from east to west. The rain was falling off, but still heavy. With a heave, Armand's body went over the side and was quickly swallowed up in the roiling green waters. They made even quicker work of Stevie's body leaving a trail of gore along the way from the shotgun blast.

Back in the cabin, Polk prodded Judge Powers with a foot.

"Madge, oh Madge, you still with us?"

There was a fluttering of the eyes and a groan.

"We need to get her ashore, Polk. It's a wonder she's alive. Look how her legs are twisted. One of them has a compound fracture, look at the bruised swelling, it's bleeding under the skin."

"She's not going ashore anywhere, I told you, I'm keeping her as a get out of jail card, if I need it."

"What are your plans for us, you heard the same things I heard on the radio. Billy's place is crawling with your buddies, it won't take long for them to put the story together and they'll have an APB on all of us. These people are innocent, they don't need to be involved. Let me at least put the dingy over the side and put the old lady, Renée, and the kid in it."

"Marcus, *you* don't understand how these things work! When you pop someone there's no going back. I've been in police work all my life and the only chumps that give themselves up are life's losers, those dumb shits that kill their wife or family. Me, I'm riding this horse all the way, dude, and I'll take down anyone that gets in my way. You, the judge, the kid . . . anybody."

Marcus knew by the madness in his eyes that Polk was serious, he was a stone-cold killer. Marcus had always played the tough guy, more out of necessity than reality. Sure, he was big and imposing and his build and brutishness had served him well. Inside though, he was still the same guy that wanted to play pro ball. When he went to work for Billy, it was his creds as a third-round draft for the Rams that locked the deal. Billy hired him on as chief of security for him and the band. As time went by, Billy cut him a piece of the action on the drug sales for handling the shipments and banking. It was easy money. When he had met Sheila one night at the Sand Bar on Duval, he flipped for her immediately. Since then, she was always on his mind. Now, the man that supposedly killed her was here in front of him holding all the cards.

"Polk, can I ask you a question, straight up, man-to-man?"

"Depends, if you're going to ask me for a loan, maybe we can work something out, with interest and a vig, of course."

"Did you kill Sheila?"

Polk's face drained of color, his right eye twitched dangerously, he said, "Now you know I can't answer that, it would be tantamount to a confession. If I said yes, and then you somehow got away, which isn't very likely, and you told my old buddies in law enforcement, I would be frog marched off to Raiford for a fast needle ride. I will say this, she was a good lay, but beyond that I don't know what you're talking about."

Marcus looked for any sign of lying, but Polk's eyes were lifeless. If he was telling the truth, then who killed Sheila? Did Billy do it? He knew everything about Billy and his crazy orgies with women and men. Maybe he got carried away and she was killed in some wild frenzy. No, Billy was a lot of things, but he wasn't a killer. It had to be Polk. Why else would he be afraid of Mikey? Maybe Mikey saw him kill his mom. That was why he was keeping Mikey close to him. The kid was never going to get off this boat alive. This was Sheila's kid, he felt honor bound to protect him.

"Any other questions?" Polk asked. "If not, let's get this skinny old broad on the bridge where I can keep an eye on her."

Chapter 23

By 1300, the storm had begun to move off to the northwest, totally opposite of what NOAA had forecast. The people with the millions of dollars of weather instruments, satellites, and major degrees of higher learning were wrong again. The storm was headed for New Orleans, like most storms this time of year. The poor folks in NOLA did what they always did when a big blow was coming their way, they partied. By 1600, it was confirmed, skies to the south were clearing, the sea was lying down, and the winds out of the east were warm and carried the smell of the sea.

The Florida Bureau of Investigation was working two major crime scenes out of a command center bus located in the parking lot of the Lagoon Motel in Florida City. One of the investigations was the prison riot at one of the several work camps located deep in the

Everglades. Work camps that were borderline slave labor camps that housed the worst of the worst that were an open secret among senior law enforcement. The body count had been rising with each hour that went by. Most of the deaths were caused by gunshot and fire. Captain Bill Price of the FBI had been working the scene all night and had returned to the command post to make his report. He was tired, hungry, needed a shave, and was really pissed off that so many of the prisoners had died while still in their thatched huts.

The other, was the developing crime scene on Shark Key that involved a major drug cache and the mysterious disappearance of the Monroe County Sheriff who was believed to be kidnapped and currently missing in action and feared to be dead. Two deputies working the location reported that their commander, Sheriff Polk entered the Key ordering the two deputies to close the entrance down and to keep all vehicles out until further word. They reported that the sheriff was involved in the fatality collision at the entrance to the Key, but it didn't slow him down. He was in pursuit of someone for sure, but they didn't know who. It appeared that he had two victims in the vehicle he was driving but didn't take the time to explain. He was the sheriff and they obeyed his orders.

"Warden Cotton, go over the events leading up to the riot again for me, please," Agent Price asked. "I'm still confused on a couple of issues that I want clear in my mind before I report back to Tallahassee."

"No problem, Price, whatever you need," Cotton said, disdain visible on his face. Who was this punk to question me? "It all started when Sheriff Polk delivered a special prisoner up from his facility in Key West. As you know, or may not know, being in the bureau and all, the jails are jammed pack all over the state and it is routine for a county sheriff to pass on some of the overcrowding on to the prison system. We get all the lifers and hard asses down here, good old boys that are eventually going to ride the needle, know what I mean?"

"I understand all that, Warden, go easy on the background, tell me what happened out there in the swamp."

"As I was saying, Special Agent Price, Polk sent a badass up here for safe keeping. I assigned him to Camp Three. Three is where I have my best men running the camp. They're tough and up to the task. Evidently, this one prisoner, Jack Marsh, started trouble the moment he arrived in the camp. He got smart with Officer Dalton and disciplinary measures were immediately taken . . ."

"Marsh? Jack Marsh? Are you saying that Polk sent Jack Marsh here? For what? What the hell is going on? I know Marsh, he's a friend of mine, a good friend."

"You'll have to ask Sheriff Polk that, Agent Price. I'm just telling you that he was brought here for safekeeping while awaiting a bench warrant from the county court. I've learned over the years working prisoners that this is the shitty end of the stick. We don't ask questions, we just obey our orders to house convicted criminals and to help the counties and state when called to do so."

"You're saying that Jack Marsh is the cause of the riot that took place in Camp Three?"

"That's exactly what I'm saying. From the moment he arrived, he was inciting the others against proper order and discipline. Officer Dalton personally called me saying he was stepping up security measures around the camp for the night. He reported that the prisoners were becoming unruly and he was thinking about arming the trustees with tasers and mace. He also wanted to put the wire up around the huts, which ordinarily was down because of the remoteness of the camp and the unlikelihood that a prisoner could survive out in the Everglades for long."

"That explains why so many of the dead were found in the burned huts. Crap, Cotton. What the fuck was this guy Dalton thinking? There's over fifty men burned to death out there, another dozen or more shot. You know what's going to happen if the press gets a hold of this? They'll be screaming for heads to roll."

"Listen, you punk, I was running prisons back in the day when pouring water over a prisoner's face was child's play. We used to drown the fuckers if they got out of line. You get your ass sent to a red-line brig, you ain't coming out the same man, believe me. I'd like to get some of these pussies in Tallahassee out in one of the camps for a few days to see what we contend with . . . these boys are all scum. They hired me to manage their human waste and that's what the fuck I do. So back off with all the holier than thou crap. My men did their jobs and they paid for it with their lives and no prissy little FBI agent is going to take anything away from them. If you're looking for blame, put it on Jack Marsh. Things were running smooth until he showed up. Hopefully we'll find his bones mixed in with all the other losers."

Price knew he was walking a thin line with this man. Theoretically, Cotton out ranked him in the state hierarchy, even though they were in different branches of law enforcement. He decided to keep his council to himself and just let the situation play out and hopefully he comes out in the shadows. But there was no doubt he was the man up the food chain responsible for so many deaths. The unknown question was why the hard on for Marsh? Did they have a history? He made a note to follow up on this angle later when he had more time, but for now there was a lot of work to do back at the camp.

Price turned to the uniformed cop working the command centers communications lines, "Get Gray on the line."

"Agent Gray speaking."

"Johnny, this is Bill, how's it going down there?"

"It gets crazier by the minute. Lots of drugs all over the place like you wouldn't believe, mounds of it on dinner plates. The CSI crew ran a quickie on the stuff and it's turning bluer than Sinatra's eyes, pure Columbian. We found the cutting room where the stuff is spread all over the place, you can't even go inside without a hazmat and a breather on. Blood splatter on one wall from a shotgun blast but no stiff. All the bedrooms are heavy with DNA, some fresh some old."

"Spare me the visuals, Johnny. Any sign of Polk?"

"None. If I had to guess, after talking with the two deputies at the entrance and the rent-a-cop, Polk had been working this case alone for a while and something triggered him to shut the place down last night. Why he went in alone is anybody's guess? I'm thinking he got popped and dumped in the bay. The tide probably carried him out and the crabs will get to him or he'll show up in a couple of days somewhere out in the bay."

"What about this Billy Rocket character that owns the place. Where is he?"

"In the wind. We hit every house on the Key and only came up with a couple of old men that live up by the gate. They didn't have much to say other than the jets flying over from Boca Chico mess with their Zen. They wanted to know since we are from the government can we do something about the jets. I told them we would get back to them. All the other estates were boarded up for the storm, everyone was gone. There could have been a bunker buster dropped on the place and no one would have known."

"No groupies or hangers on? Any servants?"

"Nope, nada."

"All right, shut it down, come on up and help me sort out this mess. It's going to take months to ID all these bodies. You're not going to believe the scene, it's one of those that will stay with you for the rest of your life."

"What about Sheriff Polk, how you want me to play this in my report?"

"Make him MIA, probability of KIA ninety percent."

"You're the boss."

Price dreaded the next call he had to make. Coco Duvalier had to be told. He was in love with Coco but was never sure if it was ever going to go anywhere. She was happy in Key West and was quite the entrepreneur under Marsh's guidance. He didn't know for sure but had seen her savings account statement once and was astonished at the wealth she had. Marsh was like a big brother to her. At times, Price hated Marsh for all of his mysterious activities bordering on criminal but could never be proven. Over the years it had become a game of cat and mouse between the two men, as time had gone by and the reports came in from down island of Jack's escapades it had become a game of chess where Jack was the Black King, and he the White night.

Bill reached Coco's cell message center for the third time, finally leaving her a message.

"Coco, I need to let you know. Jack is missing and is being presumed dead. Call me."

Chapter 24

The *Queen's* radar swept out to the horizon searching for the *Lucky Lady* off somewhere to the west of them. Bull had plotted an intersecting course assuming the *Lady* would clear the shallows of Florida Bay and turn south on a course running just off the eastern tip of Cuba. He had been wrong. The *Queen* should have made contact by now.

"Jack, can you come to the bridge?"

"On my way," Jack answered, stopping off long enough to grab a handful of crushed ice for his compress. The cold on his damaged mouth and jaw was a blessing.

"What's up, Chief?"

"I tried to thread the needle on the *Lady,* but I was wrong, I'm thinking she's running way out in the Gulf before turning south, unless she's running somewhere else. Maybe George Town isn't there target after all."

"The only place west is Mexico, why would they be heading there?"

"Tampico maybe, or Veracruz. Nothing there in either of those places, unless they plan on overhauling the craft, but why?"

Both men were leaning over the chart table in the middle of the bridge in thought.

"Coffee for you two gentlemen," Cookie said, bringing up a pot of steaming coffee and two mugs.

Cookie leaned over the chart taking a peek of what the two men were talking about.

"Seems to me that if I was on the run, the last place I would go would be Mexico. There ain't nothing there except a bunch of druggies and mean women. I was married to a Mexican once, meanest damned woman I ever met but could that girl cook."

"This going somewhere, Cookie?"

"If I was in the wind and didn't want anyone to see me, I would hide in plain sight. I would find me a busy shipping lane and get lost in the clutter."

Bull and Jack looked at each other then, at Cookie questioningly.

"You ain't the only one that's been in the Navy, Chief. I was in the brown water Navy running the Mekong in a PBR back in '66 and '67," he grinned.

"You rode a Riverine?" Bull asked, in surprise.

"Best damn M60 gunner on the best patrol boat in the best Navy in the world. I was doing fine until I let all that *Ba Muoi Ba* beer eat holes in my brain. I went crazy and shot up a sampan loaded with a bunch of monks," he laughed. "My life has been all downhill since then, but I sure lit up those gooks."

Jack laughed and slapped Cookie on the back, "Seems to me I've got the wrong man at the helm up here."

"Your full of it, Jack. The brown water boys aren't sailors at all, they're all jarheads wishing they were the real Navy."

"Watch it, Bull, you're talking to a Marine Sergeant and the swabbie hasn't been born yet that can hold a Marines dress jacket"

All three men then fell silent and focused back on the chart. Cookie picked up a pair of dividers and walked them down the east coast of the Yucatan Peninsula, close in to shore then across to Grand Cayman.

"That's your course, gentlemen," he said and walked off the bridge with the coffee pot.

Jack thought for a moment, looked at Bull, and said, "Any better ideas?"

"Not at the moment."

"Then make it so, Skipper," Jack commanded.

The storm was gone, causing havoc as it rolled north. The *Queen* was in her element, riding the waves like the workhorse she was, engines humming sending a slight vibration through her hundred-twenty-three-foot long hull. She moved inside an electronic bubble of security with her in the center as her sonar pinged the depths and her radar reached out in all directions. She was running off the east coast of Quintana Roo at twenty-two knots throwing out a four-foot bow wave as she went.

Jack's strategy was to run south along the north-south shipping lanes past Cancun, Playa Del Carmen, and then south of Cozumel, change course to 90° east for George Town. If the *Lucky Lady* was out ahead of him, he was confident that he would overtake her. If the *Queen* was running ahead of the *Lady*, then he would lay off George Town lying in wait.

His preference would be to find the *Lady* out in open water and run alongside and do what he had to do without any prying eyes, sink her if necessary then scoot back to Key West and get Luther and himself tended too.

He was worried about Luther's loss of blood from the gunshot wound and was glad Coco was tending to him with the medicines aboard the *Queen*.

"Chief, I'm going below to check on Luther, give me a shout if anything comes up."

"Will do."

The smell of onions and frying meat filled the main cabin with a delicious aroma. Jack's stomach growled in hunger as he passed the galley.

"If those are hamburgers, bring a couple down to the forward cabin when they're done. Throw in a big glass of cold milk. I'll be with Luther and Coco," Jack called out.

"Got it, two boogers and a cold milk coming up," Cookie called out.

Jack stopped in the main salon long enough to pull a blanket over Scarlet fast asleep in a lounge chair. He lingered for a moment thinking how young and vulnerable she looked and thought how dangerous the world is to the unsuspecting. One moment life is beautiful and glorious, the next, a drug-filled haze of lies and false promise.

He knocked softly on the forward berth door, "It's me, Jack." He pushed the door open and entered the large cabin.

This was his cabin under normal circumstances but when company was aboard he gave it up and slept in a crew bunk.

"How's sleeping beauty?"

"Better, I think. I gave him an antibiotic shot from the kit, lord knows how long it's been in there, but so far, no adverse reactions. I also packed the wound with sulfonamide powder, if that doesn't help heal the wound, I don't know what will," Coco said.

Jack lifted the sheet to view the wound and was shocked at the scars and raw wounds crisscrossing his back. He dropped the sheet in disgust, understanding flooded him at the way Luther had leaped onto the porch and overpowered Boss Dalton, breaking his neck and letting him fall into the mud. Luther's face had been a blank mask showing no emotion at what he had just done, payback had been a bitch.

Jack was used to death, it was no stranger to him, even as a teenager living on The Nickel, L.A.'s notorious skid row, he had killed an old wino for a few dollars. He didn't set out to kill the man, he was just going to scare him and take his money, if he had any. He hadn't expected the guy to fight as hard and only went down when his head hit the dumpster after Jack hit him with an uppercut. The whole struggle had lasted less than thirty seconds. Jack had hastily rummaged through the old man's pockets and came up with fourteen bucks. The next day he lied about his age and joined the Marine Corps and had never returned to L.A.

"Jack, what's going to happen to us? I'm so worried," Coco asked, searching his eyes for answers. "You've been involved in a lot of crazy things and I never have pushed for the details, but this one is out in the open and involves all of us. I'm scared."

"I didn't go looking for this, Coco, it came at me. Polk framed me, he wanted me to disappear, so he turned me over to that sadistic bastard Cotton in Florida City. If it hadn't of been for Luther, I would still be swinging upside down from a chain in that hell hole. I owe him big time. It was dark when we escaped last night, I didn't see the whip marks on Luther's back until just now. I know I would have gotten the same treatment if I didn't run. I know I did the right thing, I'm just sorry that so many of those in the camp died last night. If the reports we're hearing on the radio about the loss of life are correct, most of them are dead today. It was unbelievable, Coco, you can't imagine what it was like, even for just the short time. I was there. It was like being in a third world country controlled by lunatics."

Coco poured Jack a glass of water from a carafe, "Take one of these pills Jack and climb in one of the bunks, you need sleep. Everything will be okay with Bull up on the bridge and me watching Luther."

"Where's Jinx?"

"He crawled into one of the bunks a while ago to sleep off the buzz he had going."

Jack looked back down at Luther and saw that Coco was rubbing the muscled arm tenderly.

"You like him, don't you, Jack?"

"Yeah, I do. He saved my life. He told me a little bit about himself as we made our way in the dark last night. I think he's just like one of us that's been dealt a crappy hand."

"I like him too, Jack. There's something about him that brings out feelings I haven't felt in a long time."

"What about Bill? I thought you two were thinking long term."

"Bill's first love is his job with the bureau, everything else is second place. I love Bill, I guess, but our lives are so different. He never has said it outload, but I know that he has hard feelings about my past. His world is all black and white, mine . . . well, you know what I did before I met you. I'm not proud of what I did, but it was selling myself or not eating, really not a tough choice, at the time."

"Don't be hard on yourself, honey, let it go. The past is the past, you can't change it. If Bill has trouble with it now, it could fester into big trouble between you guys later."

Coco cleared a tear from her eye with a slim finger and placed a hand on Luther's shoulder, "I don't know, Jack, but I think there could be something here in this man for me. I don't know why I feel this way, call it a woman's intuition, I guess."

Jack touched her face, wiping a falling tear from a cheek. "Let's get him back to health then see how things develop. I'm going to hit the sack for a few hours, wake me if there's any downside with him."

Chapter 25

The storm had cleared earlier that afternoon and now the stars were bright across the sky. The *Lucky Lady* had ripped across the Florida straight at full throttle on a straight-line to Havana then turned west, hugging the Cuban coast. By midnight they would be off Cuba's west end and the naval base at Las Tumbas, once safely past the coastal frigates then set a course for the hundred and fifty-mile sprint down to the Cayman.

Polk had told Marcus to take the fastest route possible to George Town. The route they were on was the fastest but not necessarily the safest. Marcus had used it many times caring Billy's money down to George Town, turning around and bringing drugs back up on a reverse course. Hugging Cuba's coast was always a risk. Since their patrol routine wasn't routine at all, you never knew when they would be out guarding their shores until a bright spotlight lit you up. To conserve fuel, the Cuban Captains would lay up close into shore. If you got hit with a spotlight you had two choices, you could comply with their orders and have your boat and everything on it seized then spend a year or two in one the many prisons on the Island. Or, you could run like hell on a zig-zag course hoping you wouldn't get blown out of the water by one of the deck mounted 20mm guns. He had always taken the second course of action once he realized the Cubans were terrible shots.

Marcus was at the helm of the *Lucky Lady*, his molar hurt like hell, his eyes burned from lack of sleep, and he needed to take a leak. Another cup of Max's coffee and he would kill him. Polk had cuffed his left hand then passed the cuff through the wheel and cuffed the other end to Mikey's thin wrist, virtually shutting down any movement by either beyond the helm. If he didn't get sleep soon, he was going to collapse.

Mikey sat at Marcus's feet with his head on his knees sound asleep. The kid had finally stopped sobbing and immediately conked out. The judge was still unconscious, now with her head in Billy's lap. Billy had dozed off in a fitful sleep, his body was overtaken with the pain from his hands. Marcus still couldn't believe that Billy's hands were ruined, what a waste of such talent, an iconic virtuoso rock.

Renée hummed a song over and over as she combed her fingers through Polk's hair. They were in the master cabin where Polk had demanded she go once the *Lady* was clear of Florida Bay. He knew that Renée had been shooting up heroin with some of the other groupies and offered it her to help calm her nerves.

"Come on, Renée, I'll shoot up if you will. We both need to lighten up and get to know each other. A little ride on the dragon's tail isn't going to hurt."

"Polk, I can't, you scare me." The mention of shooting up sent butterflies churning in her stomach. The stories she had always heard about heroin always ended in tragedy, but she also remembered the euphoria it brought on. It wasn't like coke that made it feel like her heart was going to beat out of her chest. Billy had shown her how to cook-up a hit and once she had gotten over her fear of the needle she loved the instant lifting of all her troubles. She was a princess floating in a sea of rose petals.

"Don't be silly, let's have some fun, we have a few hours to kill before I have business to take care of."

She caved in more from some hidden need than any sweet talk from Polk.

Now, as they laid nude side by side in post coital bliss, she ran her fingers through his hair, humming.

"Let's do it again," she said. "I need it."

Polk's heart raced in anticipation. Renée had a beautiful body, what man wouldn't want to go another round with her. He rolled over on top of her on his knees and stared down into her big green eyes

"You like it, don't you honey. I knew you liked me. Your two snotty friends turned their noses up at me, but you, I always had that feeling that you wanted me."

"Whatever you say, but I want another hit first."

"You want to shoot up again? I thought you want to make love with me."

"No, you silly goose, I want another hit like the one you gave me before, it was so good."

Polk eyes came back in focus, clearing his mind of love making. She didn't want him, she wasn't all cuddly because of him, it was because of the shit flowing through her veins.

"You want another one, I'll give you another one, then we'll see what you want."

He rolled over to the nightstand and sat up, took a bag of coke from the drawer where he knew Billy always kept a stash of blow. He formed up a line for himself and quickly sniffed it up his nose. The hit was instantaneous, everything was crystal clear. He began to whistle as he mixed a spoon of coke with a spoon of heroin and began to stir. Satisfied that he had just put together one righteous speedball, he scooped up a spoonful of the concoction and lit a lighter under it to cook. Satisfied that it was ready, he pulled five cc's of the syrupy liquid up the barrel of the syringe, then turned to Renée.

"Come to daddy," he whispered breathlessly. His sex was huge as he mounted her. At the same time, he slid the needle into her juggler and pushed. Renée's eyes opened in shocked surprise as the mega dose hit her system. Her eyes rolled back in her head, she opened her mouth to say something, but nothing came out. Her body relaxed in death as Polk screamed and climaxed.

He lay beside her as his body trembled in fear. *'What had he just done? What was wrong with him? What was he doing? He knew he was spinning out of control, somewhere in the recesses of his mind the primordial fear of being caught made him moan. There was no turning back, all the years of working hard and building a reputation as a man of the law was gone. Over the years the self-doubt had always been there. The insecurity, the rejection was always just below the surface He remembered his father constantly telling him he was no good, he was worthless, he would never amount to anything. The old man raged that he would grow up to be like him. No one would ever want anything to do with him. He was a loser . . . a fucking loser just like his mother, the bitch whore!'*

He rolled onto the floor beating the deck with his hands and feet like a child throwing a tantrum. After a while, he regained his composure and got himself under control. He forced all the pent-up hate inside of him back in the closet where it had leaked out, padlocking it. He was born again, he was hours away from a new life, a new beginning. With the money he had and Billy's money, he could buy himself a new name and identity, a new home. He would find himself a young woman to marry and be a picture of civility. Maybe Rio or one of the islands. The world was his. Fuck his old man.

Once passed the western tip of Cuba, Marcus poured on the power. The *Lady* responded like a thoroughbred answering her jockey's urging. The morning sky was a cerulean blue with sunbeams cutting through it. A lone bird followed overhead, watching curiously at the machine below and wondering what the hurry was. The frothy waves breaking over the bow blew back in a million small diamond drops splattering the wind screen. Inside the safety of the bridge, body odor and putrid flesh cut the nostrils. Marcus was still at the helm, swaying with the fall and rise of the boat, his wrists were ziplocked to the wheel. During the night, Polk had used Ziplocs he had found in the engine room to secure everyone to a fixed part of the bridge. Billy's ankles were zipped together and attached to the chart table, Madge was linked to Mikey by the wrists then to a deck tiedown.

"Hey, Sheriff, I ain't prying or nothing, but don't you think we ought to get Renée up here and zip her up like the others," Max groveled. "I'm just saying, we leave her wandering around she could cause trouble."

"Oh, she won't be causing any trouble, Maxi, she's nice and quiet where she is."

"You want me to take her some coffee, or something?"

"I want you to shut your yap and get busy bringing all the tubs up from the engine room. Put 'em in the main salon and make damn sure they are taped tight. Once we anchor up in George Town you and I will use the dingy to carry them ashore."

"Me? I'm going ashore with you? Why me, why not Marcus. He's big and strong, me, I'm a runt."

"Because I trust you, Maxi. I've begun to even like you. You're really cute in Billy's clown suit."

Max had forgotten about the outfit he had slipped on when he was in Billy's closet a million years ago. He felt ridiculous now in the light of day. He had always considered himself a sharp dresser, but this outfit made him look like a buffoon.

"Sheriff, I'm your boy and I'll do anything you say, but number one, my name ain't Maxi, it's Max.

Number two, I ain't going nowhere looking like Michael Jackson. You just have to let me change or I ain't going with you."

"You're a ballsy little shit, Maxi. I'll tell you what I'll do. You go as you are or I shoot you right here, right now."

It took Max a split second to check all the angles and come up with an answer, "Give me five minutes to brush my hair and I'm your boy."

"That's what I thought. Now I know why Marsh kept you around, you're a useful idiot."

Max seethed at the insult but kept his mouth shut, he would continue to bide his time. If only he knew where Jackie was.

At 1430, the *Lady* eased into George Town, and contacted Cayman customs.

'George Town, this is Lucky Lady, U.S. registry requesting mooring in the harbor.'

'Lucky Lady, state your business.'

'Pleasure.'

"Are you carrying contraband of any sort? Guns. Narcotics, Tobacco products?"

'Negative, George Town.'

"Very well, Buoy eight. Pay entry fees at the customs building at the head of the shipping pier. George Town, Out.'

'Lucky Lady out.'

Marcus signed off and hung the hand unit on its hook.

"Maxi, change of plans. I've decided to take Marcus with me ashore. He knows the routine and people at the bank. It'll make things smoother."

"But, Sheriff, I thought I was your boy, don't leave me behind, I want to know the routine too. Maybe Marcus and I can both go."

"Shut up, you don't need to know anything, and don't call me sheriff anymore. He's dead, from now on I'm just Polk."

"What about your first name, ain't you got a first name. Us being partners and all, I should know your first name," Max said.

"My first name is 'shut the fuck up.' You call me Polk, that's good enough, and we're not partners! I'm going to put you in charge over these humps on the deck. Any problems, you tell me when I get back."

"You're leaving me in charge? Damn, Sheriff, I ain't never been put in charge of nuthin' except maybe my stepsister once when I was a kid and my old lady was working nights," Max said, puppy dog eyes tearing up. "I'll never forget this, I swear."

Polk shook his head at the brownnoser's mewling's and cut the zip cord from Marcus's wrist.

"Let's get this tub moored and transfer the money into the dingy, Marcus."

Max was leaning out over the pulpit with a gaff in his hands. He snagged the buoy line and slipped the *Lady's* mooring line over the dirty white ball. His mind was racing with hazardous thoughts. This was his chance to dive overboard and make his break. He was a poor swimmer at best, but with a maniac with a gun behind him, he was sure he could make it ashore in twenty seconds flat. He took his time feeding out the line, furtively stealing looks over his shoulder back to the bridge.

"Look at the skinny fuck, he looks like a subway rat on a cold pizza," Polk said to Marcus.

"He's harmless, Polk, cut him some slack. We need him working the deck, otherwise it's just you and me."

"Wrong. Once we're finished at the bank, we're coming back here to take care of loose ends." Polk said.

He pulled his briefcase from the cubby hole beneath the chart table, worked the combination lock, and snapped it open. He took his Bank of Netherlands numbered account passbook out and shoved it in his pocket along with the piece of paper he had scribbled Billy's account number on earlier while he was passed out on the deck.

'Stupid kid, tattooing something this important on his body where any freak could see it.'

He turned to Billy, who sat glaring at him holding his destroyed hands, "So, Billy in all the excitement last night I forgot to ask you what your password to your account is? I guess this would be a good a time as ever for you to tell me."

Billy struggled to sit up by inching his back up the wall.

"I know what your plan is Polk, after you get the money you're going to get rid of us, you can't leave any witnesses behind, right? You don't need to do this, you know. You can have the money but let us go, especially the kid, he's got his whole life ahead of him."

"Yeah, the problem with that is little kids grow up to be big kids, and they'll begin to wonder about their mother. Besides, you're wrong, I'm not going to hurt anyone. I'm a new man, those days are gone. I don't need to hurt anyone. After I have the account all straightened out, I'm history. You and this band of losers can do whatever you want, you'll be free to go wherever you want."

"I don't believe you. If you were telling the truth, you would take us all with you, out in the open for the world to see. After you do your business at the bank you just walk away leave us free."

"That's stupid, Billy. Don't you watch cop shows. The bad guy never takes his hostages with him to the drop. He collects the bag and then makes a call to free the prisoners. He disappears into the sunset and everyone lives happily ever after."

"Or, he gives the order to kill the prisoners. Yeah, I saw that in a 'Miami Vice' rerun."

"I'm running out of patience, Billy. Give me the password or we're going to have trouble."

"I'll give it to you if you at least let the old lady and the kid go. They're harmless."

"Harmless? Mad Madge? Are you frigging nuts, she'll hunt me down and slip the needle in herself if she ever made it out alive. No way, dude. She's first on the list to go. Little Mikey, I haven't decided yet, I just might take him with me. He would have a good life with me . . ."

"Don't you have grown son, Polk. You told me once that you wish you never had the kid. What kind of life would Mikey have?"

"Stay out of my business, Billy. You don't need to bring up my son. Now, give me the password or this conversation is over," Polk pulled the hammer back on the pistol and aimed at Billy's head.

"Elvis, the password is Elvis," Billy said.

Polk pulled the trigger, the report in the close quarters was deafening. Billy's head jerked back in a shattered mass of misty blood hitting the bulkhead then bouncing forward. His body fell to the side and was still.

Mikey screamed hysterically and hid his face in his free hand, folding his little body into a ball. Marcus stood shocked, not believing what had just happened.

"Polk! Snap out of it! Jesus, man, this has got to stop," Max yelled, as he threw open the hatchway and rushed onto the bridge. "You're killing us all. Is that what you want to do? Ya fucking punk!"

Max jumped on Polk's back and wrapped an arm around his neck and began to pummel him with his fist.

"You've fucked with us long enough, I ain't going to take it anymore. I'll kick your ass from here to Hoboken . . ."

The gunshot had wakened Madge. She was confused and had no idea what was going on. The last she remembered was running down a dark street. Where was she? What was Max Simms doing beating on Sheriff Polk. She watched in confusion, then slipped out of consciousness.

"Ya . . . fucking . . . wiseacre . . ." With each word, he would hit Polk in the head rhythmically.

Polk reached back and hit Max in the head with the pistol barrel, connecting on the second blow. Max melted to the deck, blood streaming from a gash on the top of his noggin.

Chapter 26

The plan to overtake the *Lucky Lady* by cruising the shipping lane along the coast of Quintana Roo was a bust. The only ships they saw were merchant ships owned by DOLE Fruits heading north loaded with bananas or other fruit from farther south heading for the U.S. market. The southbound boats they overtook were more of the DOLE owned vessels deadheading back for another load of produce. The waters were filled with Mexican fishing boats trawling for the oceans delicacies with their thousand-foot scoop nets dangerously out. Nets that the *Queen* skirted and avoided throughout the day and night.

At Cozumel, she turned on her new course of 90° east and made a run for George Town at full speed. The crossing of three hundred nautical miles flew by with the *Queen* under full power of thirty knots. By 1500 hours, they were in sight of George Town's port.

"Looks like Carnival Line's business is good, they have two of their monster ships tied up alongside the wharf," Bull said, as he swept the powerful Bushnell binoculars from left to right. "A couple of freighters . . . Jack! Got her! Jack! The *Lady* is anchored up in the harbor."

Jack snapped awake. He had dozed off after standing at the helm for the last eight hours. He and Bull had swapped watches throughout the trip.

"Where away?"

"One o'clock, off the bow," Bull answered pointing.

Jack focused the other set of Bushnell's and brought the sleek vessel into view. He twisted the focus nob and brought her in close.

"There's a dingy tied off on her stern. Looks like someone is loading something into her."

"I see it, some kind of crates or boxes."

"Who's the guy?"

"Don't have a clue."

"Wait minute, there's Polk."

Coco elbowed her way up to the helm, "Let me take a look." She put the glasses to her eyes and swept the *Lady* back and forth settling on the figures on the stern. "I recognize the guy. He's one of Billy Rocket's muscle guys. He comes into the Sand Bar every now and then with the little guy that they call Bones."

"What do you think, Jack?" Bull said, around the binoculars.

"Let's keep an eye on the action for a few minutes. Coco, you and Cookie fire up the wench and lower the dingy off the stern and tie her up. We might run over and get a closer look of what's going on aboard."

As they watched, Bull checked in with the port authorities and asked for the farthest buoy out from the docks. The port people were glad to oblige because everyone normally wanted close in as possible.

"They're on the move, Bull. Polk's at the tiller, and the big guy is on the bow. Let's get strapped and get over there. If we can, I want to get our people off there and get the hell out of here."

"What about Polk, don't we want him too?"

"I'll get Polk now or later, but his ass is mine. Let's roll."

"I want to go," Jinx said. Madge is on that vessel. I need to be with her."

"It's better that you wait here with the others. If she's aboard, she'll be coming back with us."

"I'm not totally useless, Jack. I know that most have a low opinion of me, but I am capable of handling myself in a tight fix."

"I believe you Jinx," Jack said, placing a comforting hand on his friend's shoulder. "Right now, I need you to keep an eye on things here board the *Queen* for me. If things go badly, you sit tight for a couple of hours. If we don't come back, get everyone ashore and back to Key West. Lock the *Queen* down and go."

"Okay, you're right, I can do that, Jack. I'll do just as you say."

"Good, now go help Cookie get the Zodiac down into the water."

Bull was at the tiller of the Zodiac as it made its way across the harbor. A hundred meters out he throttled back and drifted. Jack was on the bow with the binoculars, sweeping back and forth, looking for any movement or sign of activity. The bridge was in shadows and all the hatchways were closed tight. No one was on the bow or the stern. If he didn't know better, he would think the *Lady* was abandoned.

"What do you think, Bull?"

"Let's run alongside and go aboard, check things out."

"No, run up alongside her portside away from the customs building and I'll go aboard. You stand off and come running if you see me signal."

"Let's do it," Chief said.

The dingy nudged the port side of the *Lady* soundlessly. Jack pulled himself over the gunwale quickly and strode to a midships hatchway and started down. Inside, he pulled a 9mm Beretta from his waist band and stood silently letting his eyes adjust from the bright sunshine outside. The lapping of the harbor waves against the hull were the only sound he could hear.

He made his way aft thinking that if there were any crew members they would be in their berthing's taking advantage of the port time catching up on sleep. A quick inspection found the bunks empty. He made his way up to the next level and opened each door and peered in. One of the cabins stunk of feces and urine. The one across the hall had the smell of death. His brow wrinkled in concern, he didn't like what he was finding. Had Polk and Marcus gone completely crazy and killed everyone at sea thrown their bodies overboard?

He made his way forward to the master cabin and peeked in. The shock of seeing a nude woman laid out on the king-sized bed shook him. He crept inside for a closer look and gasped. It was Renée. She had a syringe with the plunger bottomed out hanging from her neck. Her eyes were blank with death, her lips parted as if she had something she wanted to say before she went away. Jack pulled the sheet over her body and quietly left the room shaking in fury.

The main salon was empty, the smell of overcooked coffee filled the cabin. In the galley, he turned off the burner where a percolator sat burning grounds.

He raised his pistol in alarm when he heard a shuffling overhead on the bridge. His pulse picked up, as he took one step at a time. At eye level with the bridge deck, he stopped and swept the area. His first thought was of a slumber party, the revelers having fallen in place to sleep off a drunk. When he saw Mikey, his little body curled up with an arm raised over his head cuffed to the helm, he kicked into action and took the last three steps in one leap. Nothing moved, no one yelled in surprise, the only sound was a low hum of static from the radio with its volume turned down.

He scanned the bodies. Some man he didn't know was dead, shot in the face, his blood and gore splattered against the bulkhead behind his slumped body. Judge Parker appeared dead lying next to Max whose face was caked in blood from a head wound, little Mikey sat staring at him with unseeing eyes.

He went to Max and felt for a pulse, squeezing the skinny wrist.

"Let go of the merchandise, Jackie, I ain't wearing my good watch," Max said, startling Jack.

"You're alive."

"Damned right, I'm alive. I been playin' possum ever since I heard you climb aboard. I thought you were Polk comin' back to finish us off. The man has gone bonkers. Jackie. He shot Billy right in front of the kid and the judge."

"Is she alive?" He asked glancing over to her.

A voice from the corner spoke, "I'm alive, Marsh, get me out of here and to a hospital before I croak," Madge said, her voice gravely from phlegm.

Jack helped Max up and went to Mikey. The kid was alive but unresponsive, he seemed to be in a catatonic state.

"The kid's been through hell. Jackie. I tried to shield him from all the terrible things going down, but it wasn't possible what with Polk going off the deep end and killing everybody. You had to be here to understand. It ain't been easy on me neither. When I had to toss those stiffs over the side I wept Jackie, me, Max Simms, wept."

"Stow it, for now, you can tell me all about it once we're all back on the *Queen*.'" Jack aimed the bridge search light out, aimed at Bull circling off a quarter mile, and flashed it three times. The Zodiac dingy turned and was up on plane in a matter of seconds.

A few minutes later, Bull was on the bridge.

"Who's the stiff," he asked pointing to Billy."

"Hey, ya big palooka, how about some respect for the dead. That man was a legend, a frigging legend."

"Yeah? So, who is he?"

"Billy Rocket, best damned guitar player in the world. He made Hendrix look like a punk."

"Whose Hendrix?"

"Fuck you Bull, you're busting my balls. I'm here with a headwound and I don't need your smart-ass attitude. One of these days you're going to piss me off and I'll do to you what I did to Polk."

"You guys knock it off. We need to get Madge and Renée aboard the Zodiac and get out of here."

Once Madge was safely aboard the dingy with Mikey cradled in Max's arms and Renée up forward wrapped in a blanket, Jack pulled Bull aside.

"You get back to the *Queen* and get everyone settled in. Have Coco take a look at Madge, see if she can make it back to the Keys. Shoot her up with some of the wonder drugs she found in the first aid kit, anything to make her comfortable. I think Lil' Mikey just needs sleep and quiet. Max . . . pump up his ego and he'll be fine."

"What are you going to do?"

"I'm staying here aboard the *Lucky Lady* to wait for Polk. If he comes back I want to be here to greet him."

"Jack be careful, he's a dangerous man. He wouldn't hesitate to cut your throat."

"Don't worry, Bull. I can take care of myself. I'm sure he'll be back to finish up business aboard the *Lady*. He knows he can't leave witnesses behind. I'll be waiting for him."

"I don't like it. Let's forget about Polk and get back home. There's been enough action to last us for a while."

"No, I need to see this through, Bull. If not now, I'll be looking over my shoulder for the rest of my life. Some night, he'll come at me out of the dark and I'll be a dead man."

"We need a plan, Jack. If you're staying aboard, I'll need to know what to do."

"Let's figure that he will want to get ashore, take care of his banking business, and then get back aboard. Maybe the two of them will stop for a dinner or something distracts them. Worse case, they'll be act before midnight," Jack thought out loud. "Once I've taken care of business, I'll hit you with a Bravo Six radio check, that will be the signal to crank up the engines and stand by. If you don't hear from me by first light, I won't be coming back."

"Sounds like a plan." Bull said, matter of fact. "See you in a bit." He jumped down into the dingy and was gone.

Jack watched for a couple of minutes then went inside.

Chapter 27

Jack sat in the captain's chair on the bridge eating a sandwich stacked with deli turkey and mustard slathered on it to kill the taste. He took small bites and was careful to chew on his good side. The sun had set, and the harbor was filled with long shadows and pockets of darkness. Overhead, the first of the stars began to twinkle awake, a children's rhyme played through his head, *'Twinkle, Twinkle Little Star. Wish I may, Wish I might, not get killed this night.'*

He laughed at his variation and wondered what parents would think if they ever heard their child sing such a verse. His own mother had always been too stoned to sing anything much less a lullaby. He wondered whatever happened to her, then just as quickly tuned out that line of thinking. His mother was *'Mother Green'*, the fighting machine, the Marine Corps. Everything of value in life, he had learned in the Marines; loyalty, honor, respect, brotherhood, and yes, the art of killing. He had killed several men in his life, the one that haunted him though was the old wino in L.A. He was the only one he ever dreamed about. The others were enemies of his country and he was doing his duty. Then there were others that got in is way in the world. He learned early that there were two sets of rules in life if you wanted to survive. They were the rules made by other men that think they know best what is good for others but not necessarily for themselves. The other set of rules was the rules a man laid out for himself, a sort of code of conduct, a series of red lines not to be crossed, or to be crossed. It was his decision to be made not another's. As for Polk, he needed killing. His kind didn't live by any rules, they were dervishes that whirled through life killing on a whim, no boundaries or limits. These men were a danger to everyone. They should have a bounty on their heads, with no bag limit, just an open season. But the most dangerous man of all was the one that stood afar from the field of battle and decided the rules of engagement, as the man in the field dies waiting for a signal.

The sound of a motor pulled Jack out of his reverie. He went to the starboard side porthole and watched a shadow of man hop over the gunwale and secure the painter line to a cleat. Polk stood and looked up at the bridge and smiled. Jack had the crazy sensation that he had been seen and he eased back into the shadows. He saw that the time was ten o'clock. He must have dozed off.

"Lil' Mikey? It's your new daddy," Polk called out from below.

Jack moved to the back bulkhead of the bridge next to the hatchway and waited, gun in hand.

"My little fella, daddy's going to buy you a pony."

Polk bounced up the bridge steps leading up from the main salon. At the top he stopped looking around in confusion. Where were the humps? Where was the judge?

"Max, you fuck where are my prisoners?"

"Hey, Polk. I hear you've been a naughty boy." A quiet voice called from the shadows.

Polk recognized Jack's voice immediately and staggered against the bulkhead in shock.

"Marsh!" He gasped. "It's impossible. You're dead. I heard it myself on the radio."

"Sorry to disappoint you, but I'm very much alive. I'm here to take care of some past due business, Sheriff. Something that's been needed for a long time."

He raised the pistol and aimed, center mass, taking up the slack in the trigger.

"Fuck you," Polk yelled and fell backward down the salon steps. Jack was right behind him, grabbed him by the foot before he could scramble away and pulled him in close. Polk kicked out with his free foot catching

Jack in his damaged jaw. Jaw screamed in agony, the pain adding determination in his struggle. Adrenaline dumped into Jack's stomach like a blow torch.

Polk pulled free of Jack's iron grip and crab crawled backwards, as fast as he could. Jack stood and leaped on the man taking him down. He straddled Polk's chest and pummeled him with mighty fists of rage. The loud crunch of Polk's nose shattering pushed Jack to hit harder. Polk bucked up knocking Jack to the side. The smaller man, jumped up and began kicking Jack in the head and face. Blood splattered as it opened the wounds of only a few days ago.

"I'm going to kill you this time. Marsh. I should have killed you years ago when you turned down my protection," he screamed, as he kicked.

Jack rolled away and protected his head with his hands. He reached out pulling Polk in close and squeezed him in a bearhug. They were face to face, eye to eye. Jack could feel Polk's muscles ripple in protest, he squeezed tighter. Polk's face was blood red, he couldn't breathe he began to lose vision . . . Jack relaxed his hold.

"Not so fast, Polk. You are going to know you are dying a slow death."

Polk kneed Jack a solid blow in the groin that detonated in a meteorite explosion of stars. Breath stealing pain shut Jack's mind down. Polk freed himself from Jack's falling body and hit him a judo chop to the back of the neck.

Polk searched the room for his pistol that he had dropped when he rolled down the salon stairs. His back was turned when a lamp crashed down on his head, knocking him out. When he came to, he was hanging by his feet upside down from an overhead steel girder that ran port to starboard across the salon like a giant whale's rib.

"Let me down, Marsh. Cut me down, now."

"Sorry, Polk, I want you to get a feel for what's to come. It's going to be a long night, so rest while you can."

Polk cursed and swung back and forth, his hands were tied behind him rendering them useless.

Jack was on the bridge studying the instruments, dials, and gauges of the sleek vessel. After a moment, he was satisfied that he could steer the luxury yacht. He put the two throttles in neutral and hit the starter button. The powerful motors down deep inside her belly rumbled for a moment then quieted to a hum.

"Queen, Bravo-Six."

"Bravo-Six, Queen."

"Queen, pull your hook and follow me as I pass."

"Roger, Bravo-Six. Queen out."

Jack bounced down the outside ladder and ran forward. He hit the windless start button and the powerful motor began to wind in the mooring line pulling the boat to the anchorage. Once the boat was over the white ball, Jack easily slipped the thick nylon line over the ball and the *Lady* was free. He ran back to the bridge, checking on Polk as he went.

"How're they hanging, Sheriff?" Jack laughed.

"When I get down from here, I'm going to kill you, Marsh," he screamed.

Jack spun the wheel over to 270° and moved the throttles forward. The *Lady* cut silently trough the harbors flat water with no effort. As he passed the *Queen*, Jack blinked the running lights. Bull acknowledged and turned the *Queen* to follow in trail.

At 0200, the *Lady* was fifty nautical miles from George Town. The ocean depth was eighteen hundred feet and mysterious. Jack radioed Bull to stand off and hold his position until he arrived on the *Lady's* dingy.

Jack let the *Lady's* engines turn over in neutral, allowing her to float freely on the warm calm Caribbean Sea waters. Business like, Jack dragged Billy's body down from the bridge and through the across the teak salon floor leaving a gruesome trail as he went.

"What the fuck you doing, Marsh?"

Jack ignored him, and went about his business. He swung the davit looped Billy's feet through a nylon line and inspected his work. Satisfied with his plan, he went in and cut Polk's line free from the rib.

Polk crashed down in a heap spluttering, "The fuck you doing?" he pleaded, "Jesus, Marsh, talk to me" he begged.

Jack coiled the line around his wrist and pulled Polk out to the back deck.

He looped Billy's line through Polk's and tied it off to the davit arm and began reel the line upward. The two bodies began to rise, one dead, the other kicking and screaming. Once the two bodies were up off the deck, Jack began to loop another line round and round tightly making the two inseparable, like preparing a prime rib tying the meat to the rib bones together.

"Polk, it's payback time. I want you to be thinking about what you did to Sheila and Renée. I want you to remember Deputy Kilpatrick, the night you killed him in the burning warehouse. I want you to remember how you framed me and had your buddy Cotton sent me out to that death camp. I want you to remember all the other's you've hurt or killed while you hid behind that badge. I want you to remember it all."

Jack took a long filet knife from where he had put it and began to cut Billy's body with deep cuts. The blood oozed out, soaking both men.

"I know what you're doing, Jack. Don't do it. Please, don't do it? I'm starting over. I have money, lots of money, it's yours. Look in my briefcase, it's in the salon. Swear to God, it's all yours. Listen, my money and Billy's are in my account at the Bank of Netherlands, it's all yours. It's a numbered account, just go in there and tell them I said it was okay. Give them my account number and password, they'll give you as much as you want."

"I don't want your money, asshole . . . I want revenge."

Jack began reeling higher, then swung the davit out over the water. He reached out and cut Polk's ankle tendons. Blood flowed down and over his legs and torso.

Polk was in such shock he didn't even realize what had happened. He continued to scream.

"It's yours, Jack all yours. My password is *Mother*, just tell them *Mother* and they'll give you all of it, just don't do this to me. Jaaaack!!!!"

Jack reversed the reel and began lowering the joined bodies. Once Polk's head was in the water he stopped. Polk was thrashing around crazily trying to keep his head above the water line. The blood and the commotion sent signals of trouble out to all the night predators that quickly zeroed in to the blood scent. In moments, a thrashing of long sleek bodies jockeyed for position. One moved in, tearing a piece of Billy's shoulder off. That was the signal for the food fight to begin. Jack was watching as a huge mouth opened and Polk's head was gone. Gone! One minute he was fighting for breath, the next his head was gone. Jack bent forward and threw up, he couldn't stop. The sight had sickened him. He cut the line and let the bodies sink into the primordial waters.

He went below decks to the engine room and opened all the cock valves letting sea water pour in. The bilge was full, and the engine room already had a few inches of water covering the deck as he made his way topside. As he was leaving the engine room, he spotted a tub that the lid had come unsealed. It was filled with bundled hundred-dollar bills, Jack ignore the pain in his body and lugged it topside.

He gave the tub a pitch over the gunwale into the dingy and he followed right behind it. He couldn't get away from this death ship fast enough. He didn't look back until the prow nudged the side of the *Queen*.

Chapter 28

Key West was sweltering under the hot tropical sun, the air was thick, the tourists were sweaty and stinky, and Jack was drunk. He sat at his *'Owners'* stool at the Sand Bar working his way through his fourth *'Papa's Pilar Dark'* rum over crushed ice. He hadn't shaved for several days and had no plan to for several more days. He was living on Cookie's burgers and rum. He was in a grand funk and let everyone around him know it, even the tourist that came in to drink and party gave him a wide berth, the locals stayed away. Word had gotten around that Marsh was back on the sauce, and he didn't care who knew about. At closing time, Lamont would run Jack over to his place on the back of his scooter and pour him into bed. When anyone tried to console him, he would dismiss them with a flip of his hand and a gravely, "Get Lost."

His mind played Polk's last moments on earth over and over, nonstop. When he did sleep it still played, but he had become Polk and the shark had bitten his head off. The dream played in bright yellows and darker sepias, the next night it would be in vivid blues. He knew he was going crazy but didn't know what to do. Maybe, he should take Bull's .357 mag and blow his brains out, but he would probably fuck that up, too.

"Jackie, ya gotta snap out of this funk, people are counting on ya," Max said, sliding into the stool next to Jack. "You ain't got the luxury of fucking off like the rest of us do."

Jack loved Max like a brother . . . well, maybe like a distant cousin.

"Fuck off," he said.

"Yeah, yeah, I know you don't mean it. You and I both know what happened out there on the blue. Bull thinks he knows, the judge don't remember shit and probably never will again, her memory of the whole incident is gone, Jinx was in the bag most of the time, but you and me know what really went down. I wasn't with you on the *Lady* when you met up with Polk. But I know what your disposition was towards him. He deserved what you gave him. The sweet part is that nobody knows what it was you gave him. Poof, the mutts gone, no witnesses, no proof, no body, no nuthin."

"Max, it was hard to watch. No man should die that way . . ."

"Stop with the hard feelings for him. Sheila and Renée shouldn't have died the way they did either. Sure, Billy was tops in my books, but he was dealing drugs to kids and ruining lives just as sure as he stuck a gun to their heads. What I say is, you did the world a favor. You brought us all home, we're safe, the cops ain't bothering you. Agent Price is keeping his mouth shut about that place Polk and the dude Cotton put you in. You didn't have any business in there and they know you could sue the crap out of the state if you go public. Luther never should have been in there either. The way I see it, you're clean, what's to worry about, we're free."

Jack thought about everything Max had just said, it made sense. Everyone was back safe and sound, a little beat up but alive. Max was right, but the vision of Polk dying persisted.

"A shark bit his head off," Jack turned to Max and said.

Max's expression never changed, he said, "I fucked a plucked chicken once. You think you got bad dreams?"

Jack looked at him for a moment then burst into a deep laugh. He couldn't stop, the visual of Max and a chicken was too much.

The next day, Jack came into the Sand Bar, clean, groomed, fresh clothes, a little sallow, but sober and greeted Cookie with a clap on his back.

"How about a cheese omelet, fries on the side."

Out in the bar, he spotted Coco rolling the awnings down out front. Lamont was sweeping the walkway with his earphones tight to his head dancing and singing as he went. He caught Coco's eye and motioned for her to join him.

"Well, aren't we all chipper and smelling like a New Orleans pretty boy."

Jack looked around to make sure he wouldn't be overheard, and then whispered, "I have something I want you to do. I know you can pull it off and you're the only one I can trust. There could be some risk in it, but you'll handle it."

They put their heads together and he talked for a half hour. The more he talked, the bigger her grin got.

Chapter 29

The beautiful couple had arrived on a private chartered Gulfstream jet at Owen Roberts International Airport in George Town, Grand Cayman Island at the executive terminal, recently established just for the arrival and departure of the rich and famous. A long white stretch Mercedes limo waiting for their arrival took them quickly to the Bank of the Netherlands where the bank director was waiting. Coco took the chauffer's hand waiting to help her out of the limo. Extending one of her long shapely legs on to the pavement, her feet adorned by stunning Jimmy Choos stilettos with a matching Choo Finley clutch purse. She was perfectly dressed for the part she was about to play. On a quick shopping trip up to Palm Beach's famous Worth Avenue, a shopping playground where the old money wealthy came to shop, get clipped, tucked and spent their billionaire's husband's dollars for makeovers, for the planned day she chose a snappy chic strapless Michael Korr's halter sundress that covered her full bosomed breasts. She wore a wide brimmed sheer black Audrey Hepburn style hat straight out of a scene from *'Breakfast at Tiffany's.'* The entire ensemble was, of course, in black. She was, after all, in mourning for her late husband. Coco didn't need the makeover as she was stunningly beautiful without it. But, the very handsome twosome had to play the part and did so willingly.

The bank director stepped forward out in the sun, "Madame, welcome to our islands, my name is Lars Van Venema, and I am at your service here during your visit with us. Please, come in out of the heat. Oui, our island is very beautiful, but the trade winds can mess your beautiful hair and we wouldn't want that, would we?" The man fussed busily rocking on tiptoes.

"Pardon, Moi, sir? Your name once more, please?" She cut an amusing look at Luther, now calling himself Luke.

She removed her Balenciaga metallic sun glasses and reached out to shake the director's hand, in the fashion of the rich with her palm down. The bank director was overcome with her beauty, her long thin shapely nose, exquisite make up, three karat diamond studs in each ear, and her full bosom, with just enough cleavage showing. He'd heard she was from Haitian royalty but didn't quite expect the mixture of French European with the Haitian which produced a warm chocolate complexion. She had her dark hair straightened in Palm Beach and it was now lightened to three shades of Chestnut brown, highlighted with strands of Irish Cream and various shades of vanilla frostings, cut in long layers of many textures, which, if possible made Coco even more beautiful.

Director Van Venema bowed, kissing her hand, "Non, Madame, please . . . call me Lars."

"Sir, Mister Van . . . Lars, I would like you to meet my legal counsel and banking advocate, Mister Luke . . ." The last name was not discernable, but Lars didn't question her about it. "He is here to assist me."

After recovering from his wound under Coco's constant care, Luke was able to, very comfortably, accompany her to the island for their mission. Luke was a stunning handsome man himself. He had let his hair grow a bit, no longer shaven as he was in the camp. He had a more than striking resemblance to the actor, Denzel Washington and because he was traveling incognito, now wore his beard in the fashionable five o'clock shadow, sporting a sizeable diamond stud in one ear, and a custom handcrafted signet ring by the renowned Robus

Craftsmen of London, along with the diamond bezel gold Rolex watch at his wrist. He, too, was dressed for this momentous occasion wearing a light weight Desmond linen jacket of the popular Seville Row of London, tight fitting jeans that showed off his fantastic buttocks and long legs, and a silk Valentino raspberry colored t-shirt and Bruno Magli Italian loafers. The only sign of any prison camp, Warden Cotton, or Boss Dalton and his torturing gang was from the savage scars crisscrossing Luke's back, which he made certain nobody saw now. He carried a matching leather Bruno Magli alligator briefcase with their passports, documentation, banking numbers and passwords safely tucked away and slipped his Cartier aviator glasses in the side pocket.

Lars led the way, kowtowing as they entered the luxuriously appointed bank interior adorned with Italian marble floors and Baccarat crystal chandeliers.

"Business is good, Lars?"

"Pardon, Sir? Uh, I didn't catch the name," Lars apologized.

"Luke. Just Luke."

"Certainly, Mr. Luke, as you wish. I fully understand your desire to remain anonymous. Bank of the Netherlands is the most discreet banking institution in the world. We were surprised when we were notified by Madame Polk about her late husband's death. We ordinarily never see or know our clients on a familiar basis. Once in a blue moon, one will grace us with their presence but never one as lovely as Madame."

"Can we suspend the idol chitchat, Director. I am tired and still in mourning over my loss. Let us get on with the formalities, please," Coco said.

"Certainly, Madame. I apologize for rambling, but it is not often that one of such beauty adorns our humble bank. What would you like to do first? Perhaps you would like to see the vault where your husband's money is kept?"

At the mention of her husband, Coco gave out a wail and sob. Luke went to her side cradling her elbow for support, in case she fainted.

"Yes, if we must," she whispered.

"Very well." Lars snapped his fingers and a uniformed guard unlocked a huge oak double door. The guard busied himself with more keys and locks and stood aside. Lars moved forward and placed a palm on flat screen. The metallic sound of gears and pins falling into place seemed soothing to Coco's ears and she smiled and nudged Luke, squeezing his hand.

"This side of this vault is your late husband's cash reserves. He shared this with several other clients but be assured no one is ever allowed in his cage except himself, and of course now, you."

"May I go inside and touch it?" Coco asked, coyly. Seeing so much money around her sent thrills to secret places making her steady her voice.

"But of course, Madame. I often come down into the vaults myself just to smell the money. It has a very unique smell not found anywhere else in the world. If you will pardon me, I would say it is almost orgasmic, do you not agree?"

"Smells musty to me," Luke chimed in.

"While I am here I would like to withdraw three million dollars. Would you arrange for that, please, Lars?"

"But of course, Madame. Euros, U.S. dollars, Yen, what is your preference?"

"U.S. dollars, please. I have several debts to tend to."

"Shall we go upstairs and take care of the paperwork? You have all the necessary codes and passwords, I am sure."

"But, of course, Lars."

Two hours later, the Gulfstream went wheels up and ascended into the cloudless blue sky. The flight would take them to Kingston, Jamaica where they would meet up with Jack and Bull on the *Queen*, enjoy a nice dinner in town, then weigh anchor with the three million in cash stashed in a fifty-five-gallon drum lashed to the forward deck where U.S. Customs never looked. The Netherlands account book was safely tucked in her purse with the new account number and a printed balance of US$27,485, 600 in black on the first row of the first column.

"It's a short flight, Luke. Let's celebrate with a glass of champagne, shall we? I spotted a magnum of Dom Pérignon on ice in the galley."

Not bothering to ring for the private flight attendant, Luke eased out of his seat and went forward. A moment later, he returned with two crystal fluted glasses dangling between his fingers and the cold bottle in his other hand.

"What shall we drink to, Coco?" He asked her, gazing into her brown eyes with a grin on his face.

"Hmm, how about the password to the account?" She winked at her handsome lover.

"Which is?" He asked, holding her dainty beautifully manicured hand in his.

"*Lucky Lady*, of course."

The End

Read all the Jack Marsh Key West Thrillers.

1. Key West Smackdown

2. Key West Bounce

3. Key West Drop.

4. Key West Boneyard

5. Key West Storm Warning

6. Key West DOA

Coming Soon.

Max Simms, Key West Private Eye. Loveable Max is up to his scrawny neck in trouble. Mystery with a laugh and a twist

Made in the USA
San Bernardino, CA
12 August 2019